LOVING ON A DOPE BOY

PRECIOUS T.

TEXT UCP TO 22828 TO SUBSCRIBE TO OUR MAILING LIST

If you would like to join our team, submit the first 3-4 chapters of your completed manuscript to

Submissions@UrbanChapterspublications.com

I want to shout out my amazing boyfriend, Isiah Pierce. Thank you for pushing me and showing me that there is no limit. Without you, I wouldn't have pushed myself to complete my very first book. I love you. To my mother, you're the absolute best! Love you to pieces.

CHAPTER ONE

Porsha

"*OUCH,*" *I said with agony.*

"*Stop moving, girl, damn,*" *Jermaine said.*

"*Jermaine, it hurts so bad though,*" *I cried.*

"*Baby, I got you. Do you think I would really hurt you? Just relax, baby girl. This pussy so wet,*" *Jermaine moaned.*

As Jermaine entered inside me, I began to relax like he'd told me to. After moments of long, deep strokes, I felt my body become numb. Jermaine grabbed a fistful of my freshly installed Peruvian bundles, causing chills to run down my back. As hard as he was tugging at my hair with each stroke, I felt my legs become weak, and my soul drifted from my body. I didn't know what was happening, but whatever it was, I didn't want it to stop.

"*Jermaine, ba...*" *I moaned with satisfaction, cumming all over his dick.*

Jermaine didn't stop. He kept pounding my walls harder and harder, sending my body into overdrive while I dug my nails deep into his back.

"Yes, daddy, fuck me harder," I moaned. I was starting to feel more at ease, and I no longer cared about my satisfaction. It was me who wanted to please him at this very moment.

Jermaine then turned me over while I got on my hands and knees. I followed his lead, arching my back like I'd done it before. I'd watched a lot of porn growing up and always felt left behind, considering my best friend lost her virginity at fifteen.

"Make that ass clap on daddy's dick," Jermaine said seductively.

I did something even better. I told him to lie down, and I climbed on top of him as if I knew what I was doing.

I began playing the lyrics to the song "Freak Hoe" by Future in my head as I bounced my ass on his manhood. Riding Jermaine from the back was fun for the both of us. Standing up on my two feet with his manhood still inside of me, I felt like a pro. I was doing exactly how I had seen the women do it online.

"Fuck, Porsha, I'm about to nut, baby," Jermaine said.

I said nothing as I continued. The sound of him moaning made me want to turn up even more.

"Shit, move, P," Jermaine said, pushing me to the floor. I lay there laughing as I watched him rush into the restroom to prevent his cum from hitting the floor. A little hit my foot as he scurried to the restroom. It felt so warm and sticky, but I didn't have the energy to get up and move. My legs still felt weak, so I decided to lie there until Jermaine came back with a towel. I just lost my virginity, and it was amazing. Well, at least I thought it was. It definitely wasn't how I expected it to be, but it was who I wanted it to be with, and I couldn't ask to lose it to anyone better.

AS I SAT on my bathroom toilet and replayed my encounters with my fine boyfriend, I felt my body becoming numb all over again. I remembered it all just as if it were yesterday. I really couldn't believe I had finally lost my virginity. I felt kind of lame because I was twenty-one and a junior in college. During my high school years, my parents were so hard on me and strictly about the books. The only thing was, I didn't have time to enjoy life like I really wanted to. So losing my virginity was the *very last* thing on my mind at that moment.

I had met Jermaine at a freshman welcome party my first year in college. Jermaine didn't attend the college, but he was well known around the place. I'd been messing with Jermaine on and off my whole while in school, so of course, I knew about him, but he was still a big mystery to me. Although from what I did know about him, I knew for a fact my parents wouldn't accept him as my friend, let alone as my boyfriend. Jermaine was a big-time drug dealer, the king of this drug industry. He sold everything from marijuana to the most potent crack rock on the streets. For some reason, when Jermaine and I met, we hit it off instantly, considering our two different back-grounds. Jermaine was just my type: six feet three, chocolate as hell, built like a stone wall, and tatted up like a motherfucker. I was the shy type when it came to any social outings, and I wasn't really into partying unless I was out with my best friend, Mo'Nique, but that didn't mean I wouldn't go out. Hell, it was time for me to experience the world on my own.

I could tell Jermaine really liked me, and he knew if he wanted to keep me, he would have to step his game up. I wasn't an average chick, and he knew that. Jermaine wasn't the type to settle down with just anybody though; he liked exploring his options, if you know what I mean. He was smart, graduating high school in the top 10 percent of his class, but he didn't want to continue after that. He loved the fast money, and that was something he wasn't willing to give up. I admired everything about that man.

When my phone began ringing, it snapped me out of my thoughts. I jumped up, hoping it was Jermaine, considering we'd had sex over a week ago, and I hadn't heard from him since. But when I picked up my phone and saw my mother's name flash across my screen, I was even more thrilled.

"Hey, Ma, wassup? How are you?" I asked.

"Hey, baby, I'm good. You know, still slaving over this hot ass stove for yo' daddy. I miss you," my mom said.

My mom and pops had a complicated marriage—always arguing, my dad sleeping around, and my mom was always stressing. Shit was never easy being a Wallace. I was starting to think they were just sticking together for me, but I'd been in college a little over two years now, so they could really give up the act. My mom didn't want to express her feelings to me, but I could tell my dad was still being a pain in the ass, and I hated that for her. Once I got my law degree, I was determined to move my mom to Atlanta with me. My dad and I never really got along, but that was because he never really accepted me as his daughter. He swore up and down he could only make boys. *Ha, niggas,* I thought.

"It's all good, Ma. I miss you too. Make sure you take your medicine. I know how you tend to get forgetful when it comes to that type of stuff," I said.

"I will, baby. I just wanted to call you and see when you were coming back home. I miss you so much, P, and I want to tell you something," my mom said.

"Mom, I'm coming as soon as I can. I've been working so hard, trying to pass these classes. I don't want to let you and Daddy's money go to waste. I'll try to come next month," I said.

"Well, hell, you better not. We aren't paying all that damn money for nothing," my mom said, serious as hell.

"I know, I know. That's why I want to make sure when I come down there, I won't have to rush back here to complete anything extra. I want to enjoy my time with you," I said, trying to lighten my mom's mood.

"I believe you, baby, but I'll let you go. Keep your head in those books and not into those little boys, you hear me now?" my mom said.

"Yes, ma'am, I do. I will. I love you," I said.

"I love you too, baby," my mom said.

"A'ight, Ma, call me later," I said, disconnecting the call. It was hard being all the way in Atlanta for school while my mom was in North Carolina. My mom was my rock. I couldn't even imagine something happening to her behind my no-good ass daddy. My daddy was a truck driver, and he always told me I wouldn't want a man like him, one that couldn't come home all the time. He was right. I didn't need that type of energy in my life to be honest. I needed someone that would take care of me and mine; he made up any excuse to not be with his family. I swore he did. I knew truck driving was a tedious job, but there wasn't any job on earth that would hold you hostage from spending family time with your family. He would always blame his long hours and sleepless nights on my mom and said that was his reason for cheating and dropping a check on every female that came his way every now and then. That never really made sense to me.

I honestly believed my dad used to talk just to hear himself talk. That's when I lost all respect for my dad. I stopped trying so hard to be what he wanted me to be. Shit, if he couldn't be a great father figure for me, I wasn't trying to impress him either. Before my dad met my mom, he was a true Casanova; the ladies were always all over him. Even to this day, so many old heads asked me about my daddy when I would be out picking something up from the grocery store for my mom or simply pumping gas at the gas station. I had never forgiven him after I caught him cheating on my mom in the new bed my mom had just purchased when I was a little girl. Walking in to see my dad hunched over another naked woman that wasn't my mom broke my heart. That's the first time I was ever exposed to sex. Disgusting.

I'd never forget the woman's name. Jade Marie, the biggest hoe around, had a young name but an old ass face. I wasn't going to lie though; she had a legit nice body for an old hag but not better than my momma's—period. She always walked around with that dry ass synthetic wig that looked like she should've buried it when she buried her mother. I was truly a mother's girl, and if anything ever happened to my mom, I would lose it. I needed to go see her as soon as possible. She had been begging me for almost a year now, and I just never really got around to it. I was so busy with school and trying to be involved I didn't have time.

TO TAKE my mind off of everything, I decided to get out of my dorm and take a drive in my all-black 2013 Lexus to see my best friend, Mookie. My car was a graduation gift from my mother. She busted her ass working graveyard shifts at her waitress job just to see me driving in something nice. My mom, on the other hand, had a raggedy ass 1995 Honda Accord. Don't get me wrong; those were great cars. They'd last a lifetime, but I wanted to put my momma in something newer and better. My best friend Mookie and I had practically known each other since diapers. Mookie's mom died when she was seven, so my parents decided to take custody of her. I just looked at it like she was the sister I always wanted but never had.

My mom explained to me when I was old enough to understand that Mookie's mom had been strung out bad on crack—I mean like begging on the corner. One day, Mookie and I got off the school bus to head home, and her mom was in the middle of the road, yelling loud as hell like she was talking to someone. It looked like she was fighting with the demons. The crazy thing about it was, nobody was there with her, but her mom was continuously swinging at air. Everybody was clowning Mookie the next day at school, and that's when I first saw my best friend knock a bitch out.

I decided not to tell Mookie about what my mom had told me about her mother being a crackhead, since she had already been through so much from being sexually abused by her stepdad to sleepless nights without meals because her mom would be out begging someone on the corner or just high as hell and wouldn't have the energy to cook. I was pretty positive though that Mookie discovered her mom was a crackhead when she noticed her mom falling off from earth.

Seeing my best friend was really what I needed at this time, especially after not hearing from Jermaine for a week, almost two.

Pulling up at my best friend's house already made me feel at ease with the situation.

"Hey, Mookie. Man, I got so much to tell you, girl!" I said, flipping my hair from one side of my shoulders to the other.

"Girl, I bet. Yo' ass been ghost for the past two weeks. I was starting to think something happened to your black ass," Mookie said.

My best friend was right. I had been abandoning her since I'd started spending more time with Jermaine, but I couldn't help it. He was just so damn fine. He made me want to be with him every second of the damn day just to make sure another bitch wasn't trying it.

"Girl, no! You know I'm forever good with Jermaine on my side looking over me," I said, batting my eyes.

"Looking over you? Bitch, bye. That's stalking," Mookie said sarcastically.

"Maybe that stalking shit turns me on," I said, rolling my eyes to the sky.

"Wait a damn minute. I know something is up. You're glowing today. Yo' ass better not be pregnant," Mookie said as if she were my mother.

"No, but me and Jermaine did have some bomb ass sex though," I replied.

As I was telling Mookie about the immaculate sex I'd had with Jermaine, she acted as if this shit was something she couldn't believe. But, hey, who was I fooling? I still didn't believe the shit myself, and it'd already been two whole weeks. Speaking with Mookie, I had to put her on game, not just about half of it but everything.

"Mookie, there is some shit that's been worrying me though. Me and Jermaine had sex almost two weeks ago, and this nigga has yet to return any of my calls or my text messages. His phone goes straight to

voicemail every time I call like he has my number blocked or something," I said with worry in my voice.

"Girl, it sounds like yo' ass just got tooted and booted," Mookie
said jokingly.

"Don't play like that, bitch, for real!" I said.

Just thinking about it made Mookie's joke seem to have some
truth behind it. Jermaine never went a few hours without talking to
me. Even when he was out on the block, checking niggas, he would
always contact me. I remember one time he was in the middle of
shootout, and he answered the phone. That shit turned me on so
much. Something about a hood nigga doing hood shit made me hot.
So I knew then something was up, and I needed to get to the bottom
of it. As Mookie rambled on, I pulled out my rose-gold iPhone 7 Plus
and decided to text Jermaine for the twentieth time. Man, I sure did
feel like a fiend.

To get my mind off it for a bit, I asked Mookie if she wanted to go
out for drinks. I needed it. Yeah, I had just turned twenty-one, but I
had been sneaking liquor out the liquor cabinet since Mookie and I
were sixteen. No, we didn't do it every day, just once in a blue moon.
Shit, tonight, it was well needed.

Of course, Mookie agreed, so we went and hit the outlets for
some cute shit. I hadn't stepped out in a while, but I knew tonight
was going to make up for my lost time.

MOOKIE and I decided to start getting ready for the club, and I
honestly believed my best friend was a bit more excited than I was,
and I was the whole reason we were going out. It took a total of three
hours combined for both of us to get dressed. Mookie never went out
unless she was with me, so I knew it had been a long time for her too.
Mookie was toffee brown with a slim figure.

We used to joke around about her not having an ass at all
compared to mine. Her hair was short and natural, but she kept

weave in all the time unless she had the infamous finger waves that she always wore. Tonight though, I stood there, admiring my best friend. She wore twenty-inch Malaysian hair that she had flexi rodded an hour previously, causing it to fall past the arch in her back. While at the outlet, she had bought a white dress that hugged her hips with a pair of white Red Bottoms and a small, gold Chanel clutch. Of course, this bitch thought it would be good to white it out when I told her ass not to. She never listened to me. I firmly believed white got dirty way too fast.

I felt as though I was rushing to get dressed since I had changed my outfit numerous times hours before and had finally decided on my new black pencil skirt to match the black lace top I had at home. Completing my outfit, I put on my black Red Bottoms, ready to slay some shit. I loved wearing all black; it really enhanced my shape in so many ways. I felt good. I kept my hair done in a long weave that touched the top of my ass. I had long, thick, full natural hair; I just preferred bundles over my natural hair any day. I loved my Hershey's milk-chocolate skin tone. I wasn't too light, and I wasn't too dark; I was right in the middle and had a round, plump ass and a flat stomach that complimented me.

I hadn't always been like this, body-wise. I'd worked hard for this body. I was a chubby girl all through high school, but when I got to college, my biggest decision was to boss up on everyone. Out of all the niggas who wanted me, something about Jermaine made me fuck with him the heaviest. I didn't know if it was his looks or his demeanor. I tried shaking the thought of him on the ride to the club, but I just couldn't stop thinking about what Mookie had jokingly suggested about me being a one-night stand. That couldn't be possible. My best friend and I hardly ever disagreed when it came to these niggas, but this was one thing I couldn't agree with her on.

Pulling up at Club 69, I felt a rush of excitement run through my body. I still had a thing for turning up and having fun. Tonight, I was determined to push the thoughts to the back of my head and focus on having a good time.

As we walked through the club, of course, all eyes were glued on us. All we needed was a red carpet. Mookie loved that type of attention; I swore she did. But I, on the other hand, preferred to let the niggas come to me.

"First things first, we need some liquor in our system," I told Mookie. I really wasn't a big drinker, but tonight I was.

Walking up to the bar, we immediately asked for two shots of Henny.

"Girl, we used to drink this all the time but not too much, Porsha. We know how you like to get violent," Mookie said, handing the bartender our ID's and cash.

I laughed it off because she was right. Maybe I should take it easy tonight. Immediately, I changed my mind. The last time the two of us got drunk together, I woke up in a cell for knocking Jermaine's ex, Myasia, out at the club, which had been a minute ago. That was the real reason I had to calm down on going out so much. Mookie was really my hype man, encouraging me to do everything I wouldn't want to do if I were sober.

While sitting at the bar, trying to enjoy our drinks, two fine ass niggas walked up on each side of us, offering to pay for our drinks.

At first, I was a little skeptical about this cute, light-skinned stranger buying me a drink. *But why not? I haven't heard from Jermaine in forever; plus, it's just a drink.*

I watched as this other dude grabbed Mookie by her arm, pulling her to the dance floor to dance with him. Grabbing the other guy by the hand in attempt to keep up with Mookie, I dragged him onto the dance floor with me, following right behind them. I was definitely more than tipsy.

He pulled me in close once we got to the middle of the dance floor, caressing my ass and swaying back and forth with our body's close together like someone glued us there. It felt so good to have a man's attention at this very moment. I didn't want it to stop; it could've lasted forever. It felt comforting.

Mookie, being drunk, started grinding all over the nigga like he was her personal stripper pole. I swayed back and forth with my guy until Mookie began trying to pull his pants down in the middle of the club like she hadn't had any dick in forever, which I knew for a fact was a lie.

"Oh, no, ma'am!" I yelled.

"Lighten up, P. Just have some fun," Mookie said, still trying to pull his pants down.

I rolled my eyes and grabbed my drunken friend up off her knees. I loved my best friend, and I knew exactly how she got down, but I didn't want her to get down like that in the middle of the dance floor.

"I'm ready to go," I whispered to Mookie.

I wasn't surprised when she offered to let the guys we'd just met take us home. That was just like her.

"No, Mookie. Let's catch the subway or a cab. We don't know these niggas like that," I spat.

"Stop being a pussy for once in your life, Porsha," Mookie said, heading back over to the man I had just grabbed her from. I rolled my eyes.

I stumbled to the car, and the guy I was with grabbed me and protected me from falling face forward. He restrained me, so I fell helplessly into his arms.

"My name is Vincent, by the way, and him over there, that's my brother Cal," Vince said. I ignored him. I really didn't give a fuck what his name was. At this point, I was just trying to keep from falling on my face. He carried me the rest of the way to the car. It was dark out and silent as a mouse, so it had to be no later than 3 a.m.

"I drunk too much!" Mookie yelled at the top of her lungs. We all laughed because we could relate. Finally arriving at Mookie's house, I felt so much more secure.

Man, I'm never doing this shit again. Shit is all fun and games until you start feeling the aftereffect. I thought hangovers didn't start until the sun came up, I thought.

The nigga Mookie was with, Cal, followed her straight to her room. Her ass didn't even put up a fight, but I knew how that was about to go down. Sitting on the couch beside Vince, I glared at him, trying not to make eye contact. He tried to lean in for a kiss, and I wasn't for any of that, so I readjusted on the couch, which was hard, considering how small Mookie's couch was.

"Look, I don't know what you used to, but I have a man, and he wouldn't want me entertaining some nigga," I said plain as day.

He looked at me sideways but didn't say a word, which was expected because I didn't need him talking me out of my panties. Walking into the extra bedroom Mookie had, I quickly became sad.

What if Jermaine wasn't doing the same for me? I thought.

I could hear Mookie in the next room, and she was fucking like a rabbit. I was so annoyed because it never failed with her ass. She wanted what she wanted, and by any means necessary, she was going to get it. I wanted to know what was going on. When I peeked in, all I could hear was Mookie mumbling to Cal. Weirdly, I decided to stay and watch. Mookie kept telling Cal that she was too drunk, but she knew for a fact she wanted him. Mookie always tried to low-key put up a front. I chuckled quietly as I watched as he licked his big lips in a sexual yet devouring way.

Gross, I thought.

I was surprised they didn't see me standing there with the door cracked. I didn't feel weird watching Mookie in action, because as many drunken nights as we'd had together, sometimes, I didn't have a choice.

Mookie lay on the bed with her legs open, waiting for him. It had only been a couple days since Mookie had sex, and that was why watching began to upset me. I wanted to intervene so bad, but I didn't want to cockblock. Mookie would never forgive me, so I walked away before I did something neither of them wanted me to do.

MO'NIQUE(MOOKIE)

Cal climbed on top of me, kissing my neck softly while sticking his two fingers into my wet, moist kitty.

"Ah, shit!" I whispered as Cal went in and out slowly then sped up.

Cal then whispered in my ear, "You like that, baby?"

"Mhhhmmm, I'm tired of your fingers. I want you now," I moaned. "Fuck me, please, Cal!" I screamed.

Cal was really starting to upset me with all the teasing he was doing. Cal pressed himself up against me, and I felt his soldier standing at attention for me. I wanted so badly to taste him.

As I lie there with my legs gapped open, he did something no man had ever done to me before. Shocking the hell out of me, he brought his head between my thighs, slowly kissing them one by one.

How does this nigga know all of my hot spots already?

Laying my head back on my pillow, I allowed him to explore my treasure with his tongue, French kissing it ever so softly. I grabbed Cal's head as if I were trying to pull him up, and he only refused my gesture by holding my arms down on the bed as he licked my center to pieces.

I couldn't take anymore. If Cal didn't get up at that very moment and fuck me, I was going to bust all over his face. I really didn't care, because I hoped to never see him again after tonight.

As soon as I was about to cum, Cal pulled his soldier out and deep stroked me a few times.

"Ohhh myyy gawwwd, Ca..."

Before I knew it, I had the greatest orgasm of all time, and the way Cal lay there, I could tell he agreed with me.

Quickly gathering his clothes and getting dressed, Cal gave me a kiss on the forehead and left. Not caring, I rolled over, fully naked, and drifted off to sleep.

CHAPTER TWO

Porsha

The next morning, I lay in my bed, envious of my best friend. Negative thoughts danced in my head about Jermaine being missing in action and then Mookie's drunken night. I couldn't help but compare my situation with Jermaine to Mookie's.

Was my pussy not good enough? Was it not wet enough? I mean, I sure couldn't tell with the way he was whispering sweet nothings in my ear.

I really just longed for him to hit my line. I was ready for Mookie to wake up so she could tell me about her night—well, what she remembered—also so I could figure out what was up with Jermaine. Snapping me from my thoughts, I heard Mookie in the next room, throwing up her insides. Instead of just lying there, I got up and went to get her some Ginger Ale to soothe her stomach. No matter how upset I was with her, I let it be.

Handing Mookie the Ginger Ale, I said, "So tell me about your night, honey. Spill the tea." I was looking for answers.

"Thank you so much, best. I really appreciate it. Tea? Girl, the only tea I have is, last night, I had a crazy ass dream I fucked the dude from the club," Mookie said in her goofy voice.

OK, Mookie had to be kidding me if she thought that shit was a dream.

"Well, I sure as hell wasn't dreaming last night when I heard him beating your walls down, bitch," I said, joking but serious as hell.

"Oh my God, P. I don't even remember his name," Mookie said.

I laughed and mumbled, "Do you remember any of the niggas' names you fuck?"

"What!" Mookie said.

"Never mind, girl," I said, laughing it off.

Well, that's that for finding out what happened the previous night. I enjoyed myself, but I needed to figure out what was up with my man. I didn't want to leave my best friend like that, but that bitch knew my number if she needed me.

Jumping into my car, I didn't realize I still had my night clothes on. *Fuck it. I need to see my man.* I was starting to get worried.

Slowly circling the block three times, I finally decided to pull up to the trap Jermaine frequented. I grew so excited when I pulled up and saw his car outside; then I thought, *Damn, this some stalker shit, for real.*

Climbing out of my car, I walked up to the door.

Knock! Knock! Knock!

I felt like I was beating like the police, but oh well. This was what he got for having me so worried about him. I heard Jermaine's voice and a female's laughter, so I instantly started tripping. Taedoe, Jermaine's best friend, came to the door.

"What's good, ma? How can I help you?" Taedoe asked politely.

"Um, Jermaine here?" I asked, already knowing the answer.

"Nah, he not here, but I can take a message," Taedoe said, seeming annoyed.

"Message? Nigga, you not his voicemail. Where the fuck he at?" I sneered.

Before I knew it, I was pushing the door, trying to make my way in, not realizing I managed to knock Taedoe out the way.

"What the fuck, man! Babe, it's not what you think, for real, ma," Jermaine said.

I couldn't believe my fucking eyes! Jermaine was in there naked as hell with his dick in some hoe! If I wasn't tripping, that was his ex-girlfriend, Myasia—the same bitch I had to pop at the club a few months back.

I wanted so badly to shoot the nigga dead in his head and blow that bitch's head clean off her shoulders, but I didn't have a gun. I wasn't built like that, so I did what I did best: ran. I ran straight to the door.

"Porsha, baby, come back!" Jermaine cried.

Fuck him! Who did he think I was? This man was literally my first everything, and now he was playing me. Was it really that easy for him?

When I reached my car, I hopped in and drove off with tears in my eyes, damn near causing myself to wreck. It all made sense now. That's why this lame ass nigga couldn't answer my calls. That's why he had been avoiding me. He was still sleeping around with his ex! Obviously, he thought I was just a piece of ass. I knew I should've curved his ass when I saw him at that party, and none of this would've happened.

That shit tore me up inside.

Driving back to Mookie's, I couldn't do anything but cry, pulling over at least three times to clear my tears so I could refocus my vision on the road. I was beyond ready to tell her what was up. I knew my bitch would be on go! She had warned me about his no-good ass, but I wasn't trying to listen.

I sat on Mookie's couch, crying my damn eyes out. I was lucky she was there to keep me calm because I really could've killed his ass. That was how much anger I had.

A part of me wanted to hear him out, but another part just wanted to say fuck it. A nigga was going to be a nigga.

Mookie told me she'd found the dude's name and number on her nightstand, so she decided to hit him up so he could remind her of what happened the previous night. We both laughed hysterically when she told me she didn't even remember him giving her head.

"It must've been good because I'm pretty sure I came all in his face, the way his lips tasted when he kissed me. I can't believe I can't remember that, but I can remember how a damn weak ass kiss tasted," Mookie said.

"Wow, Mookie, you really missed something you'll never get again. You know it was a once in a lifetime thing for you," I said jokingly.

"Bitch, at least my man wasn't fucking some hoe in the bando," Mookie said.

I laughed because it was actually funny seeing his naked, bare, black ass fucking a bum like some fiend. She probably owed him some money for some crack or some shit. It was always rumors in the street about Myasia. I tried to ignore them, but when I heard she was doing crack, I took that shit and ran with it. So what if it wasn't true? She was a hoe. Something was telling me to just hear him out, but tonight wasn't going to be the night I heard from him, because anything he would've said would've sounded like a lie to me right about now.

"Girl, bye. He's blowing me up as we speak," I said as if that made the situation any better.

"P, put his contact on 'Do Not Disturb' so whenever he hits your line again, you won't pay it any mind. What he did wasn't right, and it wasn't no justifying it, period," Mookie said rudely.

As the night went on, Mookie and I watched *Pretty Little Liars* and ate popcorn. Eventually, both of us dozed off.

The next morning, I woke up to Mookie damn near burning the house down because the bitch couldn't cook to save her life, but she swore up and down she could. I walked into the kitchen, taking over.

"Move your ass out the way," I said. She did what I asked her to because she knew she didn't know what she was doing.

I made us both cheesy eggs the way we both loved them, along with brown sugar sausage, a side of grits, and pancakes.

"Damn, P, these pancakes taste just like how Momma used to make 'em. I was trying to wake you up to breakfast to try to make you feel better, but you see how that turned out," Mookie said, shoving the food down her throat like she hadn't eaten in years.

"I learned from the best, boo," I said with confidence.

I finally decided to check my phone and had forty missed calls, fifteen text messages, and ten voicemails from Jermaine.

"Damn, Mookie, this nigga Jermaine was blowing my shit up last night. Ole girl pussy must be wack as hell," I said, laughing it off. Deep down, I was happy because he really cared for me enough to make sure I was straight, regardless of the situation. I took no time replying to his numerous messages.

Me: I'm really mad at yo' ass, but something is telling me to let you explain.

Less than two minutes later, he texted back.

Hoeboy: Babe, I'm so sorry, you know I love you. I have to explain all that shit to you face to face, even though I know you probably don't wanna see me.

The nigga was right; I didn't want to see his ass. As soon as I did, I would fall into his trap and forget everything that happened, but I still decided to meet up with him and give him the benefit of the doubt. My dumbass.

Me: A'ight, Jermaine, we can meet somewhere. How about dinner tonight at that new spot? You can pick me up at 7 from Mookie's house.

Hoeboy: A'ight, ma, I'll be there.

I knew changing Jermaine's name in my phone had to be the pettiest thing to do, but at that moment, I really didn't care, so he was going to continue to be addressed as a hoe until he learned how to tighten up. I didn't know why I was so hype, but after all, I did miss him like hell. The way he held me and kissed me, I just missed everything about him. No matter how hard I tried to be mad at him, I couldn't. This nigga put a spell on me.

Meeting with Jermaine low-key meant everything to me. That was my baby, man. I didn't know if it was me, but the feelings seemed to have grown between us since we'd fucked. I didn't mind, because I knew Jermaine felt the same way. But now, I was second guessing everything because if he really loved me, he wouldn't cheat. Jermaine knew the background with my mom and dad; he knew what my dad took my mom through and how I felt about the cheating, lying, and games, but still, he found a way to hurt me.

When Jermaine came to pick me up, I made sure I had on my best outfit. I wanted that nigga to see what he had lost even though I didn't really plan on leaving him. I had a soft spot for the man. Our bond really couldn't be broken, especially after I gave him my virginity. I always told myself the man I gave it to would be my husband, no matter what.

I'd decided to wear my Peruvian hair straightened with denim high-waist pants that hugged my ass ever so tightly with a soft-pink crop top, pink Michael Kors clutch, and black flats. I wasn't really trying to overdo it, but I did want him to recognize a real bitch when he saw one since he had missed the memo the first time. I checked my phone and had a text from Jermaine

Hoeboy: Bae, I'll be there in 2 minutes.

I didn't reply. I just decided to come out when I saw his car lights. Jermaine had decided to drive his white Rolls Royce. I wasn't a fan of this type of car, but shit, he made anything look good. The whole ride there, Jermaine blasted Kodak's "Like That" through the speakers. He knew that was my favorite song, and I knew every damn word.

I was going to be stubborn tonight, but it was kind of hard because Jermaine had on a Polo Ralph Lauren sweat suit, looking extra daddyish. I wanted him so bad, but I had to play hard to get. It took us no longer than twenty minutes to get to the restaurant. We pulled up near the curb, and Jermaine jumped out and ran to my side to open the door for me. We walked toward the restaurant, allowing the valet to park the car.

Inside the restaurant, nobody was in the building but the host, waiters, and cooks. I knew Jermaine had something to do with it being empty. This was a new Italian restaurant that had just opened, so for it to be empty was odd.

"Damn, it's kind of dead for it to be a new spot, right?" I asked jokingly.

But Jermaine only replied, "Hell yeah." He looked as though he had something up his sleeve, but I hadn't figured it out yet.

Once the waiter directed us to our table, I got sick on my stomach for some odd reason, probably just some late aftereffects of the liquor I drank the previous night. I took a sip of some water and brushed it off. Jermaine wasted no time explaining himself to me. I was mad he jumped right into that, but then again, I was ready to know why he had played me for a lame bitch.

"Babe, I'm 'bout to explain myself, and I don't want you saying anything until the end. A'ight?" Jermaine said.

I looked at that nigga with a screwed face like, who the fuck did he think he was, demanding me and shit? I rolled my eyes and said, "A'ight." Jermaine knew it was hard for me to keep quiet during an argument; that's probably why he suggested I be quiet 'til the end.

Jermaine began speaking. "A'ight, bae, listen. At first, I didn't hit you up for a few days, because I was trying to get my mind right and shit. I know I was your first, and I wasn't really tryna take on all that responsibility like being in a relationship and shit, because I knew that's where we were headed. Then I realized I really love you and couldn't do you like that. I can't even imagine you throwing that good ass pussy to another nigga. I started thinking about our future, our families... but then, on the other hand, I also realized we cut from a different fabric, ma. I'm not trying to turn you into something you don't wanna be, but I need a shorty by my side that's 1K and willing to bust at a nigga if I need her to. I want to be with a girl that can hustle like me and get to the bag like I do, no questions asked, and I know you ain't built like that."

I sat there, looking dumb as hell. Was he saying he didn't want to fuck with me like that because I wasn't built like him? Did he think Myasia was more fit for the job? I mean, he did tell me she cheated on him. How the fuck was that holding you down? Niggas were dumb as hell.

No this motherfucker wasn't sitting here, blaming me for what the fuck he had done. I started to get up and walk away. I really couldn't take any more of his bullshit, but he grabbed my arm.

"Man, I'm not done yet, P. Hear me out, man," Jermaine said.

For some reason, I sat back down, regretting that I had ever done so.

He continued. "That morning you walked in on me drilling that bitch, it was because I was drunk. I don't even fuck with Myasia hoe ass like that, and you know that. I'm not gon' sit here and blame the liquor for all my actions, but that's some of the reason things happened the way they did. She called my phone up, asking me for some weed, and I told her where she could find me. Me and Taedoe was just sitting in the trap, drinking and shit, and she came in all aggressive, feeling on me and shit. I don't know, man. Something just came over me. I should've fought that urge, I know, but it was hard. I'm not gon' bullshit. I haven't been in a relationship since her. When Taedoe answered the door, I didn't tell him to tell you I wasn't there. I heard you at the door. I was just in a fucked-up situation, ma."

I felt tears creeping into the corner of my eyes.

I can't believe this nigga, man. Why did I even come out to eat? I should've just left his ass begging like the dog he is.

"Don't cry, ma, please. I know I fucked up, but if you willing to give me another chance, I'll never get caught lacking like that again wit' some broad. I won't even think about another bitch as long as I'm with you. I didn't mean to hurt you. You gotta believe me," Jermaine said.

I believed him because, when I looked into his eyes, he looked genuine and true to his word, but I couldn't fix my lips to say anything. I felt broken all over again but this time worse. I guess they were right when they said the truth hurt.

We ate in silence. Of course, Jermaine kept trying to break the silence, but I was too hurt to speak.

I DIDN'T REGRET GOING BACK to Jermaine's house after dinner, because I did want to forgive him, but I just couldn't fix my mouth to say it. I felt so dumb, but if loving him was wrong, I damn sure didn't want to be right.

Lying in bed with Jermaine felt like where I needed to be, but I couldn't sleep at all, because I kept thinking about how I'd seen him with that girl. What was wrong with me? Why couldn't I just get over it? It shouldn't be that hard, right? Did I need a therapist or some shit?

Lying there, I began thinking about what he'd said about needing someone who was willing to bust at a nigga if he needed them to. That really wasn't my lifestyle, but it was crazy what love would make you do. I was considering breaking out of my shell just for him.

I felt the warmth of Jermaine's body against mine, and it began to take me away from my thoughts. My ass was on his shaft, and for some reason, I felt myself becoming aroused.

Stop, P! I was trying to tell myself to calm down, but apparently, Jermaine couldn't sleep either. He leaned over and kissed me, making everything so much sweeter. Our tongues began to wrestle one another as he sucked my bottom lip, and that shot me through the roof.

I hated that I got turned on by the smallest things, especially right now, but I wasn't going to fight this; I missed him. I rolled over on top of Jermaine, sitting on top of him. Our bodies connected like glue, and I felt him getting hard, causing me to lick my lips.

Jermaine said, "You know I love you, right, P?"

I smiled. I couldn't say yes, because if this nigga loved me, he wouldn't have cheated; he would've controlled himself, liquor or not.

I leaned down, kissing his lips, making my lips moist so when I planted my kisses on his neck, knowing that was Jermaine's weak spot, he wouldn't know how to act. I knew all his spots already, and we'd only had sex one time.

Jermaine cuffed my ass in his hands, squeezing it gently, and I reached down and began massaging his manhood.

"You like that, daddy?" I asked in my sexiest voice.

He moaned, so I knew he didn't want me to stop. I pulled his boxers down, and still holding his manhood, I licked the tip, teasing him a bit.

"Mmmm," moaned Jermaine.

I was going to teach his ass a lesson. I stuck all nine inches into my mouth and sucked the tip, my jaws locking on him.

Jermaine moaned even louder. "Oh shhhhitttt!"

I got up, pulled his boxers up, and rolled over.

"What the fuck are you doing, man? You just gon' play with me like that, P, for real?" Jermaine asked.

Indeed, I am.

"You don't get that pleasure until you learn to think with the head on your shoulders and not the one between your legs. Period," I spat.

Jermaine sat there, feeling dumb as hell before running to the bathroom to finish what I had started. I found it funny, and listening to him in the bathroom made it even funnier, but he was going to learn his lesson.

I lay in his bed with a devious smile on my face, waiting for him to come out of the bathroom. He was taking forever to come out, so I finally drifted off to sleep. I was content with not letting him play in the cookie jar until he learned how to act accordingly.

Jermaine

Sitting on the edge of the bathtub, my thoughts began to race. Man, I couldn't believe I fucked up that bad with Porsha, man. She meant the most to me. Then again, I couldn't believe she was out here playing mind games with me. That was not even her, but I guess I deserved it. I swear I was going to make this shit up to her if that was the last thing I did. I loved that girl with all of me. I just couldn't lose her.

Washing my hands, I walked out of the bathroom and laid back on the bed next to Porsha. Cuddling her close, I kissed her forehead softly, wrapped my arms around her, and tried to get some sleep.

"We'll get through this, baby girl," I whispered.

Lying next to Porsha, I just knew this was the girl I wanted to spend the rest of my life with. We might have had our ups and downs, but what relationships didn't? I never knew we were going to make it this far, but as long as I had her by my side, I would never jeopardize that. Ever.

CHAPTER THREE

Porsha

I had woken up before Jermaine, so I decided to cook. His ass usually slept in late as hell, and I wasn't about to just sit here with a growling stomach. He had a nice ass appetite too. I remember when I used to sneak that nigga into my room, and he would eat all my damn snacks. My mom always questioned me when I would shoot her a text saying I needed more snacks so soon.

"I hope you aren't getting fat down there or feeding two," my mom would say.

Jermaine had a nice townhome on the westside of Atlanta, and it was really low-key. He had five bedrooms and three bathrooms. I liked it. There was more than enough space for both of us although I wasn't always over here. It took him a long time to even show me where he stayed. It felt good though, just walking around in one of the big ass T-shirts he had given me last night. I felt so at home, and being out of that dorm room and away from my aggravating ass room-mates put me at peace. For some odd reason, those bitches and I never got along, but I knew it was because of whom I was fucking with. Jermaine had a lot of bitches on his dick, but as he said last night, he only wanted me. That's why bitches were mad.

While cooking, I decided to make Jermaine a plate and do breakfast in bed, which he liked. I mean, shit, I could still pamper my man. There was nothing wrong with that. When I finished, I took Jermaine his food, and he kissed me with his smelly ass morning breath like he always did.

"Nigga, you didn't even brush yo' teeth yet and already tryna stick yo' dirty ass tongue down my throat," I said, laughing.

"Ma, that's that real love. Don't play with me. That was some fuck shit you pulled last night tho'," Jermaine said, speaking on my freaky tricks I'd done on him the previous night. Jermaine always wanted to get to the point; he never really sugar-coated anything. That's why I was surprised when he started being distant instead of just telling me what was up.

I laughed. "What are you talking about? Oh yeah, when I rolled over on that ass." We both laughed like crazy.

"Jermaine," I said.

"Wassup, baby?"

"I wanna talk about what you said last night at the restaurant," I said, ready to dig in his shit.

"OK, go ahead."

"So what did you mean exactly? Like, you want me to drop out of school and shit and become yo' assistant? That shit is not happening; that's what you got Taedoe for!" I said, mad as hell, remembering each and every word he'd said to me last night.

"Nah, ma, I didn't mean that at all if that's what you thought. I just want you to be my main lady on some hustling shit. We get this money together, some Bonnie and Clyde type shit. When I say go, you on go," Jermaine said.

"Nigga, I'm not yo' do-boy! What the fuck?" I said, rolling my eyes.

"Bae, listen. What I'm saying is, I want you to be in school and shit, getting yo' degree if that's what you want to do, but I want you to be able to hold shit down when I'm not around. Like when we have kids and shit, a muthafucka' run up in here and I'm not home, you check that shit," Jermaine said, summing it up for me.

I hadn't even thought that far, but I loved the sound of Jermaine and me having kids.

"So, babe, what you want me to do?" I asked.

It was easy for me to submit to my man, but this nigga needed to be on his shit, or all of that would be out the window.

He explained how he wanted me to sell his drugs from his house because he sold to his best customers from his house, meaning rich and white with good jobs. The people who wouldn't hurt me; they just got their stuff and left. Broke motherfuckers got the trap house experience. I didn't know what I was getting myself into, but I agreed, and Jermaine smiled.

I wondered if I should tell Mookie. *Nah. That's just some extra shit for her to gossip about.*

We sat on the bed and went over drug shit until I had it down to the T.

PORSHA

I had this shit down pat. I was selling to high-class people since Jermaine said he didn't want me working out of the trap house; he had people to do that for him. I was pretty confident in what I was doing, and he had taught me how to scale it and bag it properly. I found myself spending more time at Jermaine's house and even had clothes and shit there now. I really didn't mind, especially if Jermaine didn't. He was barely there though. I spent a lot of my time there because it was a break from being on campus. It was a good thing we were on break from school because now I didn't have to worry about going back at all. I saw why Jermaine loved this fast money. It came in so quick. Shit, I loved it too. I didn't want to give it up, and I had just started. It was so addicting, having my own money and being able to buy my own things.

I pulled up to Jermaine's crib in the new pink Porsche Jermaine had gotten for me, and of course, he wasn't home. It didn't matter though; I wasn't really expecting too many plays today. I had become content with being there alone most nights although it did get lonely.

I cruised into the yard, opened the garage, and began pulling in, what she didn't notice was someone watching me on the other side of the street. I popped the door open and walked into the house, ready for business. I didn't even know I had this street shit in me. I was so business savvy.

Maybe I should've gone to school for business instead of law. Law was all right and all, but there was too much that came with it. Plus, I was only doing it for my mother. If I could make money how I was making with Jermaine, I would do this trapping shit for a lifetime.

Jermaine said it turned him on how good I was, and it didn't even take him long to get me right. I was a fast learner. I was really just trying to make daddy happy, which, of course, made me happy. Jermaine had put me in a position to win; that was the least I could do. Mookie said I shouldn't have agreed to this lifestyle, but who cared? It was 'secure the bag' season, and I wasn't being left out. I was tired of asking my momma and daddy for shit. Mookie didn't understand that though since she had her own job. Mom told Mookie that if she decided not to go to college, then she would need a full-time job. But Mookie's ass worked just enough to get her a place, and she quit. I didn't have that option. My only option was to go to school and pass. But I was really on the verge of calling it quits anyway. I was making perfectly good money with what I was doing, and school didn't get me here.

When I settled in the house, I heard someone beating on the door like the police. The fiends usually did that like it would make me rush to the door. But it was rare. I thought it must be a customer, but I didn't know why the hell they hadn't used the damn doorbell like a normal person.

Crackheads already got me fucked up early this morning. It's never that deep to get a hit, or maybe it is for them. I snatched the door open with an attitude, noticing it was the dude from the club I was with the other night. Why the hell was he here?

For some reason, my voice got caught in my throat, but that didn't stop him from speaking first.

"Aye, ma, I know you know who I am. I'm not here to hurt you. I'm just looking for that bitch ass nigga Jermaine."

I quickly went into defense mode, voice shaky as hell but trying to sound legit. "He not here, nigga, so you can fucking leave if you ain't buying nothing!" I spat.

"Bitch." He punched me in my jaw, and it immediately started throbbing.

"I said I wasn't here to hurt you, but you not gonna talk to me like I'm some bitch ass nigga."

I lay there on the ground, struggling to catch my breath because he had nearly knocked the wind out of me. I couldn't believe he had put his hands on me. He wasn't the same sweet and innocent looking nigga from the club.

This was exactly what Jermaine was talking about when he said I needed to be able to hold shit down. I was really in a fucked-up situation.

Vince walked in, and behind him followed a voice similar to Cal's.

What the fuck is going on?

The other dude held me down, while Vince cuffed my hand behind my back. All of the drugs were sitting on the kitchen counter.

I was expecting some big-time buyers today. How could I let this happen?

Vince began talking to the other guy. "Make sure she don't move, and grab them drugs over there, man, while I search this place for that nigga."

I watched the masked man put everything we had left in the bag. I looked down at my pants, trying to see if I saw my phone in my pocket, but I didn't. This was when I needed it and Jermaine the most, and neither were around at the moment.

How could I leave my phone in the car? Oh my God!

After about five minutes of searching, Vince discovered Jermaine wasn't there, and I wept.

Man, I wasn't built for this lifestyle, and I knew that when Jermaine told me what he wanted. I should've told his ass no right then and there, but no; my ass wanted a check I knew my ass couldn't cash. Ugh.

"Since I can't find him, we'll take his girl. That'll make that man come out of hiding," Vince said, looking at the masked man.

"My nigga not hiding from y'all bitch asses!" I yelled.

Vince snatched me up by my arm. He was so strong. Why hadn't I noticed this before?

He walked closer to me and spat, "Bitch, what I tell you about talking to me any kinda way?"

He jabbed me hard as hell on my right side, and it felt as though he had crushed my ribs into tiny pieces.

"Oh, you not so tough no more, are you, ma?" Vince asked.

"Fuck you!" I sneered.

"Mmmm, feisty. That shit is a turn on," Vince said seductively. He walked even closer to me, licking my earlobe in a slow motion that made my skin crawl.

I snatched my head away from him, and he looked at me with a devious smile and grabbed my ass.

"I'll deal with you later. Let's go, man," Vince said.

The masked man swiftly grabbed me off the ground, damn near dragging me out to the car and throwing me in the back seat.

I didn't know why they felt the need to do this now, but he blind-folded me with a black bandana. I couldn't see anything, nor did I know where we were going, but I already knew one of the niggas and didn't mind telling Jermaine if I ever saw him again.

Remembering that it was dark outside when I pulled into the driveway of our home, I was sure no one had seen me being abducted. Plus, Jermaine barely had any neighbors. I was in a really fucked-up situation and didn't know how things were going to look for me in the end, let alone how I would get away. I felt an anxiety attack coming on, but I just took a few breaths, trying to bypass it.

How could I get myself into this mess?

I still couldn't believe this nigga had really snatched me out of my house like that. He was really bold because Jermaine was really with the shits.

I assumed we had arrived at a house because they walked me down some steps similar to walking down into some sort of cellar.

Vince whispered in my ear, "It's OK, baby girl. You just gonna stay here for a bit. If you act right, then you can leave." He said that like it was a good thing. I hated this nigga, and I didn't even know him.

When I got down there, he threw me on a mattress that smelled like ass and must, and I heard another girl whispering. He took my blindfold off, and I saw a brown-skinned girl that favored Jermaine a little too much. She was wearing raggedy clothes, and her hair looked a mess.

Vince yelled, "Shut up! Didn't I tell you when you're in my presence, you stay silent? Meet Porsha; she's here for a little bit, so make her feel welcomed."

I looked around the dirty room, disgusted, arms still tied behind my back. My arms began to feel sore, and I asked if he could take the cuffs off, but he told me no.

The girl looked at me and smiled once he made his way out of the tiny basement. I smiled back. I had so many questions I needed answers to. Like, why the fuck were we smiling, and how long had her ass been down here?

Little did I know, we both had some relation to Jermaine. I later discovered the other girl's name was Chelsea. She was Jermaine's little sister, and she had been in the basement for nearly three years. I couldn't believe my ears. Three whole ass years? What the hell?

Apparently, this nigga Vince had an ongoing beef with Jermaine, and it hadn't just started with me. Little did I know, Vince had been watching my every move since I'd started messing with Jermaine my freshman year in college; he had pictures of Jermaine, Chelsea, and me with a map taped on the wall with lines connecting different dots. I didn't know what any of this meant, but how the hell did I get involved? This nigga was creepy as hell! I knew something was up with Jermaine because he never opened up to me about his personal life and his family. I had a feeling he was holding out on something, but I didn't know it was this deep. My mind roamed as I tried to piece it all together, but nothing was making sense. I had let this nigga Vince catch me lacking, and that's all there was to it.

As I sat down in the basement, talking with the girl I now knew as Chelsea, she provided me with all the information I needed and answered any of my unanswered questions. I was very appreciative of that since her brother couldn't put me on game. Chelsea was Jermaine's biological sister, and she hadn't had any contact with him since a year before her disappearance. She told me she and Jermaine met through a private investigator. Jermaine had someone paid to find her. He didn't even know they lived in Atlanta. Jermaine was the oldest between him and Chelsea. She was only eighteen. She told me how Jermaine was adopted by his best friend Ace's family. Chelsea explained to me how Jermaine was the only boy, and her mom simply didn't want any boys, so she gave him up to the first family that showed some sense of care. As she was explaining to me Jermaine's background and their family issues, I felt tears stinging at my eyes. Everything was starting to make sense now on why Jermaine was so private with his life. It was sad.

Chelsea then explained the night of their kidnapping in depth to me.

"I was out at the club. I originally went there for drinks only. Then I was heading back home until Vince fine ass came up to me and distracted me. He offered to give me a ride home, seeing that my Uber never arrived and I was stranded alone. When I got in the truck, there were three other guys in the back, but I didn't think anything of it. Niggas always travel in packs. I just wanted a ride home."

"So you mean to tell me you just got in some truck with some random ass niggas and didn't think anything was suspect about that? Why didn't you just call Jermaine?" I interrupted her. This story was already starting to piss me off because she was acting as if she didn't have common sense, and I even knew that—to call someone I knew before hopping in the car with a bunch of niggas.

"I didn't call Jermaine, because I wasn't trying to hear a lecture from him. I was having fun until everything went left. He's so over-protective of me. Even though he barely knew me, he still considered me blood, and he treated me just like his little sister. When I met Jermaine, my life changed. Before, I didn't have to worry about looking over my shoulder. We already felt like caged birds with our mom. We just needed space from the both of them," Chelsea replied.

At that moment, I didn't need for her to tell me anymore. I was just piecing two and two together in my head with every bit of infor-mation they gave me. I felt for Jermaine. His situation was so similar to Mookie's, minus the drug addict of a mom, but it explained why he moved the way he did. I felt like if I didn't know him before I met his sister. I really knew him now. I didn't even need her to explain to me why she'd gotten in the car, because honestly, with my parents' strict guidelines, I knew exactly where she was coming from. Holding a kid hostage from the world and sheltering them would only make them lash out and be wild.

Chelsea continued explaining to me while I sat in silence and took everything in.

"Vince asked me to chill at his crib for a bit before he took me home, and I agreed. I ended up getting too drunk, a simple careless mistake," Chelsea said.

"Rule number one, never get too drunk around people you barely know!" I said.

"I know now. I hadn't been out the house in forever, so I was really just trying to enjoy myself without thinking about every little thing. I began to feel spaced out after I took a few sips of the drink Vince handed me. The room was spinning, and I remember not being able to keep my balance. He had to put something in my drink. When I woke up, this is where I was. I feel as though I let my brother down. Although I had nothing to do with the situation at hand, I broke every rule in the book. I'm supposed to be the strong one, be careful of my surroundings, and always stay alert, the one to notice who Vince was. I know my brother has a lot of haters, and he's widely known in the drug industry and the streets period. Too many niggas are trying to knock him off the map for me to have this dumb ass slip up. I should've known, man. Jermaine used to tell me stories about people trying to set him up but not succeeding. I just thought he was joking. I didn't know he really had people on his head like that. This world is so cold." Chelsea began crying.

"It's not your fault, Chelsea," I said.

"All of this beef and animosity, I just knew it had something to do with my brother. Niggas really couldn't stand Jermaine. Yeah, they showed respect when he was present, but niggas really envied him because of his connections and the money he had."

"They confiscated my purse with my phone in it, and I wasn't able to contact anyone for real this time," Chelsea said.

"They?" I asked.

"Yes, some nigga named Cal. I don't think we've ever seen him before," Chelsea said.

Cal? Why did that name sound so familiar? The nigga from the club. I knew it was his ass underneath that damn mask.

"After a few months, I just stopped trying because he had Cal to come down here almost every night to inject me with some shit, preventing me from being able to fight back. Then I would've been out of here. I swear to God. I'm not talking about a drug that just knocks you out for a couple hours; it had me stuck for weeks at a time. I had gotten so sick once. I was foaming from the mouth, and he denied taking me to the hospital. He gave me one water bottle each time he came down here, enough to keep me hydrated and alive. I must have a strong immune system because I beat that shit. Thankfully I didn't die. I just prayed when I could that someone would come save me," Chelsea continued with tears still in her eyes.

"Oh my God, are you serious?" I couldn't believe what she was telling me; it was starting to make me sick. This is some shit you see on Lifetime, not real life. Hell no! I can't go out like that! We won't go out like that! God has a weird way of making things happen, but I'm sure he sent me here for a reason, and this will be our last night in this bitch.

This nigga was weird—sick fuck. Jermaine had trained me for this shit, and I was going to use it to my advantage.

I sat on the cold, hard concrete ground, replaying what Chelsea had told me about Cal being weak and not able to handle his own. If it was the Cal I thought it was, I was really going to lose it.

Suppressing the thoughts, I immediately began brainstorming how we could get away. Chelsea and I sat for about an hour, trying to come up with a plan of escape. It was time, and she agreed.

I had a bobby pin in my hair, holding my messy bun intact, so I removed it, letting my hair fall. I wrestled with the lock on the hand-cuffs for a good five minutes before I actually got it unlocked.

I knew Vince wouldn't be back down until the next day, and it had to already be late as hell. Now that it was two of us, we knew we could get away easily, and that was exactly what we planned to do.

Once my hands were finally freed, I decided to look for some-thing that would help me attack him. Of course, I already knew how to shoot a gun because Jermaine had taught me how; he just hadn't gotten me my own gun yet. We just hadn't gotten around to it yet with both of our busy schedules.

The only thing I found in the dusty, rundown basement was a hammer. I didn't exactly know what I would do to escape, but I knew when I saw that nigga, I was going to beat his damn head in like a piñata.

I hid the hammer under the jacket I had on when I first got there. I pretended to use the jacket as a pillow so when Vince, Cal, or whoever came down here, they wouldn't suspect anything.

"Tomorrow is the day we get away. I'm not playing. Just how we practiced," I said to her.

"We got this," Chelsea said.

We heard footsteps coming toward the door, and though we didn't move, we knew it was time. I pretended to be sound asleep, and I told Chelsea to stay up. She reminded me so much of Jermaine with her smooth, chocolate skin and big head. She had numerous tattoos on her arms with semi-long box braids that were screaming to be taken out, but I didn't say shit, because I already knew what she had been through.

When the man entered the room, Chelsea warned me that it was Vince by rubbing her nose. I had one eye open, watching his every move, waiting to catch him slipping.

He walked over to me and spat, "Wake up, bitch. I know you ain't sleep."

I didn't move, hoping he would go mess with Chelsea like planned, but he didn't. Instead, he kicked me hard as hell in my stomach, causing me to gag. I looked up at him with nothing but anger in my eyes.

"Yeah, I knew your thick ass wasn't sleep. Why you keep playing with me?" Vince asked, licking his lips. I was so disgusted and decided to make my move and give her the signal to follow me.

We assumed he was alone because no one else had come down with him.

I reached under my jacket, grabbing my hammer, going straight for his manhood, causing him to fall to the ground, screaming in agony.

"You stupid bitch!" Vince cried.

I got up and laughed. "No, you stupid bitch."

I took the hammer and began banging him in the head like a damn piñata.

Watching blood leak from his head, I felt like I was about to vomit. This wasn't me at all, but I mustered up a smile and ran out with Chelsea following me. When we got outside, we noticed his all-black Tahoe parked near the house with the door wide open, so we quickly ran to the truck. I decided I would drive since I knew my way around Atlanta, and I knew the way to where we were going.

When we approached the car though, I noticed a body in the front passenger seat. It was Cal. I didn't want to hurt him. I looked him over and didn't see a weapon on him, so I decided it would be best to keep him alive. I mean, he was my best friend's boo, and he didn't seem like a troublemaker, just a nigga trying to get some money. I felt bad for his sad-looking ass.

I knew Vince was very manipulative, so I thought it would be best to hear him out after all. Once we got on the road, I smacked his face, waking him up. He looked scared as hell when he saw me driving and not Vince, but I didn't give a fuck. He needed to start explaining because what they had done to us, especially Jermaine's sister, was too cold.

Finally pulling up at my best friend's house, I walked in her front door. She always kept it open like she lived in a safe neighborhood or something. Mookie lived in the projects, but she swore up and down nobody would ever think about robbing her. I found Mookie in the bathroom, and I couldn't believe what I saw her doing. She was sitting on the toilet, crying. Not just crying but bawling her eyes out. As much as Mookie had been through, I'd never seen her cry—ever. I quickly ran to her side and discovered the pregnancy test sitting on the edge of the bathroom.

Mookie was pregnant and didn't know what to do because she didn't know Cal that well to have a baby with him. He was the only possible father because the nigga she slept with before used a condom and pulled out too. I tried to comfort her by holding her, but she was hysterical. I told her that Cal was sitting in the car and wondered if she wanted to explain to him or if she wanted me to do it. Knowing my best friend as well as I did, I knew she wasn't the type to handle those kinds of situations on her own.

Mookie decided that I'd been through enough this past week, so we could wait to tell him together tomorrow.

"Fully rehearsed," Mookie said.

"Rehearsed? Bitch, this ain't no play. Just let him know he gon' be a daddy," I said.

"What if he isn't ready, P?" Mookie cried.

"Bitch, if this man nutted in you, he's more than ready, and if he not, he gon' get ready!" I said.

This bitch was really worried about how a nigga felt when she had a whole baby in her.

"Girl, your focus isn't on him no more. It's on this baby and what's best for him or her. Tomorrow, I'll take you to the doctor, and we're going to get you some prenatal pills. But right now, you're going to relax a bit."

CHAPTER FOUR

Porsha

The next morning, Cal explained to us that he didn't even know Vince like that. They just worked at the same company at some warehouse in Downtown Atlanta.

"Vince promised me so much cheese, man. He told me if I helped him get out of a situation he was in, he would pay me a good percentage. He knew that Jermaine was the biggest drug dealer around, so he saw him as a come up," Cal said.

I looked at this motherfucker because he had some part in this, and I wanted to get to the bottom of the situation. "So you mean to tell me he really thought holding us hostage would bring him money?" I asked.

"Well, honestly, yeah. He had this shit planned out to a T. He would call Jermaine and put up a ransom for half of his drugs and ten thousand dollars. He was going to set Jermaine up and make him think he was going to give him his sister back at the drop, but he was really planning on killing Jermaine," Cal said.

We all sat silently, listening to Cal.

"Honestly, I didn't want to continue with this nigga much longer.

He told me it would be fast money, but after a few months, I knew this nigga wasn't close to catching Jermaine. I never had any beef with the nigga. I just wanted some chip," Cal said.

Just the thought of my boyfriend being shot down made me sick to my stomach. I couldn't even grasp what he was saying. I didn't even want to picture Jermaine in a casket, let alone being set up by some square ass nigga. I was glad I did what I did, and I didn't regret it one bit.

The night Vince was killed, Cal had already planned out what he was going to do, but I beat him to the punch. Apparently, Vince had slipped something in his mango Arizona on the way to the spot, causing Cal to pass out. Cal said the only reason Vince did that was they got into a heated argument before they arrived to us.

"I told that nigga he was on some bullshit. He wasn't even doing what he said he was gon' do. I told his ass his idea with holding y'all hostage was sick. I wanted out, but this nigga said he would kill me if I didn't follow through."

That explained why he was knocked out in the passenger seat when the girl and I stepped into the car.

Once I retrieved my phone, I realized I had many missed calls and text messages from Jermaine. My baby missed me, and, of course, he was worried, but little did he know, I had handled everything that needed to be handled. Everything else, I would leave up to Jermaine.

Me: Babe, I'm good. I have a lot to explain to you about some shit that went down. I also have your sister Chelsea with me.

Baby: My sister? Really, bae! Y'all meet me at Hibachi Cafe on Carnegie Way.

I was so happy to be free. Although it hadn't been long, it felt good to finally be on the way to see Jermaine.

"Y'all, let's get ready to go meet Jermaine at the Hibachi restaurant downtown," I said, and we got up and exited.

"Let's go!" Chelsea said with excitement in her voice.

I could tell she was the most excited. It seemed like it hurt her the most to have let Jermaine down, and I hated she felt that way.

JERMAINE WAS OVERLY EXCITED when he saw me and his sister walk into the restaurant.

"Believe it or not, man, I've been looking for you for a minute now," Jermaine said.

Chelsea smiled. "I know, J. I'm just upset yo' ass didn't move a little quicker. Instead, you let yo' girl beat you to the punch. Literally," she said jokingly.

We all laughed as we ate the Japanese food he had already ordered for us. Surprisingly, he knew exactly what I wanted. Hibachi was my favorite thing to eat.

Chelsea began to speak, her voice hoarse like she needed some water. "So, J, I know I met Porsha already in a bad ass situation, but did you ever plan on introducing her to me? I mean, from what she said, y'all been rocking for a minute."

Jermaine laughed. "Yes, man, of course, I was gon' introduce y'all. Y'all really the only family I have in the A, man, besides Ace and his peoples. Her, man," he said, looking at me. "She's something special. I wanted to wait until the right time to make things official between us."

I was pretty impressed. Jermaine had seemed distant, and I knew there was something about him I couldn't quite understand. It was like a missing piece to a jigsaw puzzle. I knew the piece came in the box, but I just couldn't find it until I met his sister. Then everything was so much clearer. I just looked at him, admiring him for how strong he was and how he kept it together. He was a whole different person to me.

We all sat around the table, laughing and telling jokes. Some of the stories, I couldn't relate to, because they were about their childhood. I cherished the moment because I felt so close to them, but I still couldn't shake the thought of my best friend being pregnant; it was really getting to me.

With Mookie being pregnant, I swore I felt like she was making the wrong decision at the wrong time. I mean, she hadn't even finished school, let alone started her career. But I wasn't going to knock my girl if that's what she wanted to do. Babies were a blessing, and who was I to judge?

It was a cold winter night, and Mookie had invited Jermaine and me over because she wanted to cook dinner and chill. She knew damn well she couldn't cook for shit, but we still came anyway to spend time with her. Ever since we'd been held hostage, Jermaine didn't want me out of his sight, but I needed some fresh air, so I agreed.

Sitting in Mookie's kitchen at the bar, I drifted off into my thoughts as I always did.

I low-key needed a break from the drug shit for a little bit. I mean, it took Jermaine no time to get me back right, and this time, I was aware of everything, and nothing was stopping me except school starting back in January. My mom occasionally called, telling me how sick she was. I just assumed she missed me and wanted me to come home for the holidays, but I couldn't run the business from North Carolina.

I heard Mookie calling my name, breaking me completely out of my thoughts.

"Damn, P, you couldn't hear me with them big ass ears you got!" Mookie yelled.

"Bitch, shut yo' ass up. I heard yo' fat, pregnant ass," I snapped.

Mookie was barely four months, so she wasn't that big, but I wasn't used to seeing my best friend with a round stomach.

Cal kept talking to Jermaine about getting down with him, and Mookie even considered it, but there was no damn way Cal nor I was letting her put herself or the baby in that situation although she swore she could handle it.

For some reason, Jermaine thought it was OK to let this nigga tag along with him and know all the ropes to what he did. I, personally, wasn't feeling it. I knew Cal was a snake; I got that vibe from him instantly. I didn't give a damn if he was my best friend's baby daddy; he wasn't shit. I mean, technically, Mookie was a one-night stand.

I stood over the hot stove, making sure the roast was fully done and tender before adding potatoes and carrots on the side. Mookie boiled the water for the rice, and she damn near couldn't do that right.

"Mookie, how do you expect to have a family, and you can't cook?" I asked.

"I don't plan on cooking for that nigga or a family," Mookie said sarcastically.

"What, Mookie? You sound crazy as hell. Girl, you 'bout to have a baby soon," I said.

"Well, you can teach me then, Chef Boy R Bitch," Mookie said.

We both laughed hard as ever.

"I love you, Mookie, and you know I'll never lie to you, so when I say this, believe me. Bitch, teaching you how to cook would never work. You slow as hell," I said jokingly.

"I'll learn. Can't be that hard," Mookie said.

Mo'Nique(Mookie)

I was standing in the kitchen, stirring the rice, thinking about this whole baby situation and having a family. Was I even ready for this? Could I handle all of this? My biological mother didn't even raise me. Tears began to fall down my face because I was too overwhelmed. I didn't even notice Cal walk in. I was all caught up in my feelings.

"What's wrong, bae? I can tell something is up," Cal said, kissing my neck.

I didn't know why, but I was so easily aroused now since I had gotten pregnant. I mean, my sex drive was high before, but now, my God!

"Nothing, babe, just thinking about our little family, you know? I just worry. I don't want to be like my mom, not having a man around to help me and support the baby and me," I said.

"Baby girl, I swear you'll never have to worry about that. Now since I'm down with Jermaine, we'll be on top before you know it," Cal said with a smile on his face.

I stood there, looking in his eyes, becoming wetter and wetter by the minute. I'd never had a man to be so loving and one who actually wanted to help me.

"Daddy, I missed you," I said sexually, whispering in his ear.

Cal moved closer to me, caressing my breasts and sucking my neck.

"Mmm, baby, not right here. Not now," I pleaded for him to stop, not really wanting him to.

I knew Cal and I were long overdue for this, but I had to put it to an end. Good thing I did because as soon as it got hot and heavy, Porsha walked in. We quickly dismantled from each other, looking crazy like two high schoolers getting caught.

I couldn't help but laugh. Porsha was on to us, but I didn't care too much.

When Porsha walked in, Cal immediately walked out.

"Damn, he really likes me, Porsha," I said.

"He barely knows you. It's kind of weird," Porsha said.

Porsha was right. Maybe I needed to take a step back and try to see it for what it really was. Well, what was it really?

"OK, let's eat, everyone. The food is finally done," Porsha said.

Of course, Cal and Jermaine came running. We all sat at the table and ate until we couldn't eat anymore.

"Well, I'm going to call it a night," I said. I was really full, but I was ready for dessert, and I wasn't talking about the famous cheesecake Porsha made either. Cal and I departed from the table and headed to the bedroom, while Porsha and Jermaine cleared the table. I loved my little family.

JERMAINE

As I was cruising down the highway in my all-black Tahoe. I couldn't shake what Porsha had told me last night about how she didn't trust Cal, and she didn't like how he moved. Despite what he did to P, I felt like he was manipulated into doing some shit he didn't want to do. I was always down for giving second chances. I felt like nobody was ever really there to give me a second chance, so why not look out for somebody else who was in need? You'd do anything when you needed money, and that's a fact.

Cal really didn't give me an off vibe after he explained his part of how he came across Vince, Porsha, and Chelsea. I felt like he was being honest and true, but then again, I wasn't too good at reading people. Ace would always tell me that having a good heart would lead to me being zipped up in a body bag one day. He told me shit like it was, and he wasn't up for sugarcoating a damn thing.

I had to make a quick phone call to my homeboy Ace and let him know ahead of time that we had big moves to make so he could be prepared. Ace had been my best friend since middle school, and we practically did everything together from fucking bitches to getting money. In school, everyone thought we were real brothers because we favored each other so much.

I remember in high school, I was on the verge of being kicked off the basketball team for selling weed to some of the prep kids at my school, and Ace took the fall for everything. I remember feeling so bad for letting him take that suspension for me. It could've been worse, but Ace's mom and dad were one of the biggest donors of North Atlanta High School.

He was down for anything although he didn't like getting his hands dirty unless somebody crossed him or me, and I'd never had somebody like that on my side before. I was grateful for him because he kept my ass out of a lot of shit; he was my personal peacemaker. Picking up my gold iPhone 7 Plus, I dialed Ace's number and waited for him to answer.

"Yo, Ace, what's good with you, man? I'm 'bout to pull up on you so we can make some moves, playa," Jermaine said.

"A'ight, my nigga. Ya know a lot of our chip been coming up missing ever since you recruited that new nigga. That's why I'on fuck with new niggas," Ace said.

"Not too much over the phone, my nigga. We gon' handle that. Be ready when I hit you," Jermaine said.

"A'ight, bro," Ace said, ending the phone call.

I was really trying to give this nigga Cal the benefit of the doubt, so I really wasn't trying to point any fingers right now.

Ace and I decided to chop it up at IHOP since we were already meeting Valentino, our plug, there. It was our favorite little spot to meet our plug. It was mandatory that Cal tagged along even though after the news I'd gotten, I really didn't want him around. I followed protocol, walking in as if nothing was on my mental. I was pretty good at that, considering all the shit I'd been through in my life.

Walking up to the booth where Valentino Hernandez was sitting, I was more than ready for this meeting because it was time for me to take on more work, which meant more money. Valentino talked as we listened. He always kept shit short and sweet, and good for me today. I wasn't feeling too long-winded myself.

"You sure you prepared for this, J?" Valentino asked, looking at me.

"Hell yeah, man. This is just what me and my people need. You know I'm good for it," I said.

"I trust you, J. I know you won't fuck the pack up, but next time we meet, I want you to come out to my house and meet my family," Valentino said.

"I'll never let you down, and sure thing, my nigga. Just tell me a date and time, and I'll be there. You know that," I said with urgency. I'd never been outside of the States, so traveling to Cuba was something I was down for.

"We'll speak more on that later. Here's a bag. In this duffel bag, there is over two million dollars' worth of product. This is the most I've ever handed you. Don't let me down," Valentino said, serious as hell.

"I gotchu," I said.

Valentino handed me the bag, and we exited the restaurant. "Until we meet again," Valentino said as I walked out the spot.

Valentino had been my plug for years. I met him through an old business partner—Hood. I couldn't really fuck with that nigga Hood like that, because he was too messy, but none of that mattered, because when Valentino met me, he wanted to fuck with me on this drug shit more. I looked up to him because he was where I wanted to be in life in the near future. He had a beautiful ass family, a nice ass house, and many cars. He didn't even have to lift a finger; he had niggas like me across the world working for him.

We were taking on more drugs, and the more drugs, the more money, and the more responsibility. Although this was something big for my guys and me, I couldn't help but think about Porsha's feelings about Cal and how her gut feeling was never wrong. I started feeling a bit leery about the meeting we'd just had because I really didn't feel comfortable with Cal knowing all our business, but I let that slide, trying not to let Porsha's comments back into my head.

Although I should listen to P, I'd take my own advice and hope for the best. I guess it was just in my character to continuously look out for people. When I was younger, my mom completely abandoned me and threw me off onto another family, and I still found someway in my heart to seek forgiveness. I never understood how someone could just neglect their own child. I literally remember having a mom, and then the next day, I was going to stay with a whole different family. Not a family that I wasn't familiar with but a family that wasn't really mine.

That didn't stop me from getting this money. I allowed my mind to shift back to the situation at hand because thinking about my mom and her fucked-up ass choices only made me more upset, and now I had someone I could take it out on. I guess it was time for me to realize that not everyone could be as good of a person as me.

I had seen Cal hit the bag a few times, which didn't bother me much, but rule number one was to never hit your own supply. That was one thing I didn't support, because I didn't play about my money, period. I had no problem going back to a two-man army. I'd get to the bottom of his real M.O. because what's done in the dark always comes to light.

PORSHA

Jermaine and Cal swore up and down they had so much business to handle as soon as we woke up, so they couldn't enjoy breakfast with us. I was still trying to figure out why my boyfriend was acting like he couldn't sense Cal's bullshit a mile away. When Cal explained his story about how he and Vince had come about, there were too many holes, and it really wasn't adding up to me. Just because Mookie was fucking him didn't mean they had to be cool.

I really didn't mind them leaving, because Mookie and I had a lot to do too as far as picking out baby names, and today was her appointment to figure out what she was having.

I kissed Jermaine goodbye and told him I loved him. I knew what Jermaine was doing wasn't good, considering it was illegal, but Jermaine was already in too deep. I hated that there were so many people that wanted to see Jermaine dead. One thing I did know was that he was always careful with the moves he made. Well, at least I hoped.

After we ate, I decided to hop in the shower first. Mookie only had one bathroom in her small ass apartment, and I hated coming over because she always wanted to rush me out the bathroom or come in while I was still getting ready.

Mookie yelled, "Don't be in my shit all day! My doctor's appointment is in two hours, hoe!"

I laughed. Mookie had a great sense of humor, just like me, and I thought that was why we got along so well.

After grabbing my black Dolce & Gabbana sweat suit and lace red thong, I ran to the bathroom. When I walked in, I saw Cal's phone on the sink, unlocked. He must've forgotten it here. I didn't trip, but something told me to go through it, and I saw a message from some nigga named Louis. I scrolled up, only seeing two messages, assuming the rest had been deleted.

Cal: Yea. Bro, that nigga Jermaine gon' get what he deserves.

Louis: Oh. I already know. Tonight still on go, right? I already been finessing money from this dumb ass nigga.

As I read Cal's message, it just confirmed everything I'd been saying all along.

I couldn't believe what the fuck I had just read. Cal was going to try to set Jermaine up, and he didn't even know it. I knew this nigga was a snake. My immediate reaction was to call Jermaine and tell him what I had just seen, so I called Jermaine four times but got no answer.

"Man, what the fuck!" I screamed.

Mookie ran to the bathroom door. "You good, P?"

I had to play it off. I didn't want to tell her before I told Jermaine, because her ass would try to defend him, and I didn't want to hear all that.

"Girl, yeah, I'm good, just cut myself shaving," I cried.

"I been told you to shave them hairy ass legs. See what happens when you don't." Mookie laughed.

I heard her walking away, but I still couldn't get ahold of Jermaine on the phone, so I texted him.

Me: Bae 911. I been trying to call you.

Baby: What's good, ma? You know I'm handling business.

Me: I seen Cal texting some nigga named Louis, telling him how he been finessing you and asking him was tonight still a go.

I sat there for a total of four minutes, waiting for a reply. Jermaine was taking forever. I low-key already knew something was up with him.

Baby: It's all good, I'ma handle that tonight. Love you.

Me: Love you too. Be safe, babe.

This shit felt like a dream. Jermaine was too nonchalant about certain things, and I could never figure out what he had in mind. I swore it was always something with these niggas. I just hoped Jermaine prepared for whatever went down.

Baby: I guess this what the fuck I get for recruiting a new nigga I barely know. I knew better than this shit. I need to handle Cal, and whoever this weak ass Louis nigga is.

I loved when he talked street to me; that shit was so attractive. I lusted over the text for a moment before replying something simple when I really wanted to say fuck that nigga and what he had going on; I needed some dick.

Instead, I replied.

Me: Bae, just handle it and leave it at that.

I didn't receive a text back, but it was fine. I knew Jermaine could handle his own. Mookie saw that I wasn't really focused on the doctor's appointment, and she began to get upset with me.

"I'm sorry, best friend. There's just a lot going on right now, but you have my full attention," I said.

"P, thank you for being here for me when nobody else was. You didn't have to do that, but you did, and that's why I love you, and I want you to be my baby's godmother." Mookie smiled.

"As long as I'm walking this earth, I'll be here for you and that baby regardless. I love you too, best friend. Now let's go get these vitamins for Baby Mookie," I said, laughing.

I knew it was wrong for me not to let Mookie know what was going on, but she didn't need that stress on her at this time. The timing wasn't right.

CHAPTER FIVE

Porsha

I finally arrived at the doctor's office with Mookie, and everything began to feel so real. I couldn't believe my bestie was really having a baby. As disappointed and upset I was, that all went away when we entered the OB-GYN's office. The pale white walls were decorated with pictures of newborns all over. It instantly made a case of baby fever take over my mind. I'd never thought about having a baby before—well, of course in the future but nothing too soon. But seeing my friend so happy and nervous at the same time made me want to feel the same feelings. Just thinking about her happiness and how much joy that would bring her made me want to feel the same thing. Don't get me wrong; I was more than happy for her, but I longed to feel that happiness as well. My time would come, for sure. No doubt about that. So, for now, I was just going to be by my best friend's side and try not to let my emotions control my thought process.

———

"I WISH we would've left earlier. If I knew your ass was gon' have me constantly pulling over to let you pee, I would've left three hours early and skipped washing my ass," I said, rolling my eyes.

"Well, bitch, if you wouldn't have been talking all day, then we wouldn't have this problem," Mookie spat. She was right, but I didn't give a fuck. I kind of felt bad about not telling her about Cal's wishy-washy ass, but whatever.

Sitting in the waiting room, waiting to be called, I became anxious. It took the nurse no time to call Mookie back.

"Monique Grace?" The nurse called Mookie's real name, and she quickly jumped up. She seemed more excited than I thought she would be. I was more nervous than she was. Mookie had to take the top half of her clothes off and replace them with a gown. While waiting for the doctor to come back, I decided to break the silence and lighten the mood.

"So what you are hoping for, Mookie?" I asked her.

"Honestly, I want a girl so I can show her the relationship I always wished I had with my mom, you know? Well, my real mom," Mookie said, referring to Janice, her biological mother.

"Well, I was hoping for a boy if that matters," I said, laughing.

"Nah, it doesn't, bitch," Mookie said, laughing. We heard a knock on the door, and in walked the doctor.

"How's everything going, Ms. Grace?" Doctor Winter asked.

"Good, Doc. I'm just ready to know what I'm having so I can share the news with my loved ones," Mookie said, trying to sound white as hell. I chuckled.

"Well, let's get started," Dr. Winter said.

As he began applying the ultrasound ointment to her stomach, I felt the urge to step out and call my mom just to check on her, but I held it back. I hated doctors' offices. When I lived in North Carolina, I always had to rush my mom in for her high blood pressure. My mom was always forgetful of taking her medicine, but she was really careful with what she ate. Every time I brought her in, they would always need to admit her so they could keep an eye on her. I didn't know why I had gotten so worried suddenly, but I couldn't miss this. I made a promise to myself to call my mom later.

"Well... Ms. Grace, you're having a baby girl! Congrats," the doctor said.

"Yessss. That's exactly what I wanted too. I prayed day and night for this moment," Mookie said with excitement. I was so happy for my best friend. I kissed her forehead and congratulated her.

When we left, I decided to call Jermaine, but he texted me and told me he was handling business. He was always handling business, and he rarely had time for me. I rolled my eyes at his message. Mookie and I decided to go shop since we knew what the gender was now.

Jermaine and Ace

"I knew this nigga was up to no good, bro," Ace said.

"I know, bro, but what I got planned, ain't no returning for his ass," Jermaine spat.

Ace thought it would be a good idea to take that nigga Cal to a little cabin we had rented outside of Atlanta and do his ass dirty.

"That's a bet," Ace said.

Ace followed me in my truck. I told Cal we were going to the trap because I wanted to show him a few things before we headed back home. I made him believe I was going on a little break and wanted him to take over. Of course, he believed me.

Dumbass nigga, I thought.

When we arrived at the trap, Cal jumped out first, not noticing Ace behind him with a shotgun. Ace took the butt of the shotgun and knocked Cal out, leaving an enormous gash in the back of his head. He fell to the ground, grunting before he went unconscious. Ace and I dragged him inside and tied him up. I didn't even want to ask the nigga any questions; I believed every word my girl said, and I knew she would never lie to me. With Cal's body drooping over in the chair, I shot him three times, sending bullets through his brain, causing blood to splatter over the wall. Ace was my right-hand man, and I didn't trust anybody in these streets but him, so I knew I had nothing to worry about. We dragged his body out to the woods nearby and burned the cabin. Ace poured gasoline outside, and it went up in flames, and we walked off.

"That'll teach a nigga not to ever fuck with our money, bro," Ace said with a stern face.

I nodded. "Hell yeah. Aye, bro, why don't you come by the crib and meet Porsha's best friend? She gon' need somebody to keep her mind off that other nigga," I said.

"Shit, I wouldn't mind playing step daddy with Mookie's fine ass," Ace said, and we both laughed.

When we arrived at the crib, we told Mookie that Cal had told us to let her know we had dropped him off with his friend Louis. Mookie's faced scrunched up, but she didn't care. She just wanted to share the good news with her baby daddy, considering they both wanted a girl.

"Well, for what it's worth, you guys, I'm having a girl! Baby Mookie in the house," Mookie said happily but not as happy as she could've been if her baby daddy were there.

Ace took that as his opportunity to make a pass at Mookie.

"Congrats, ma. I'm sure she'll be as beautiful as you are," Ace said, shining his pearly whites at Mookie.

Mookie smiled. "Thank you... and your name again?" Mookie looked at Ace as if she was undressing him with her eyes.

"Ayden, but you can call me Ace," Ace said, still smiling.

"Nice to meet you, Ace," Mookie said seductively.

"All right, you two, calm down," I said. I wanted Ace to get acquainted with her, not try to fuck on the first night.

Mo'Nique(Mookie)

Two weeks had gone by, and nobody had heard from Cal. I began to get a little worried, but I found myself pushing the thought of him out of my head. I was very vulnerable, and the time spent with Ace was more comforting than I thought it would be. He was starting to come around a lot more and spend more time with me than Cal and I had spent in a full two weeks. I felt myself starting to catch feelings for him. I knew it had only been two weeks, but for what it was worth, he was a really nice guy.

We all sat around my fifty-inch flat screen TV, watching the news and playing board games, our typical family night. Ace and Jermaine decided to pick at least two days out of the week to kick it with us at home outside of their busy lives. Being with these people really made me feel happy, and I had even started to glow from my little baby girl.

I froze in my tracks when I saw Cal's picture flash across the screen as one of the dead bodies found on the outskirts of Atlanta this morning. Crying hysterically, I fell to my knees. This couldn't be true.

I saw Porsha look at Jermaine, and he gave her a strange look.

Hurt and devastated, I immediately turned the TV off.

"No. No. No. This can't be true. Why me?" Mookie began asking us as if any of us could give her an honest answer.

Porsha

I went to comfort my best friend. I knew this would be a tough time for her, but I knew we would get through it together. We'd been through way worse, and if it were up to me, I wasn't going to let this break Mookie. I helped her up from the floor and onto the plush loveseat in our living room. Ace, Jermaine, and I all sat on the ground, holding her as if we had just lost a close friend.

As I held my best friend in my arms, I couldn't believe what I had heard on the news either. I knew there was something fishy going on when Jermaine and Ace came back to the house without Cal. I knew Jermaine was ruthless but not this ruthless. Something about that nigga turned me on even more.

Eventually, we got Mookie to go to bed with the help of Ace. I knew Mookie wouldn't mind letting him sleep with her; that's just how easy she was. Being the great friend I am, I didn't judge her, because I knew for a fact this was going to be a tough time for my best friend. I felt like I was holding so many secrets from her, but I couldn't let them ruin our friendship. Not ever. I loved her too much.

I walked into the guest room at Mookie's house, which I could now call my own because I basically lived between her house and Jermaine's.

"Bae," I called out to Jermaine.

"Yes, baby," Jermaine whispered back as he led me to the California-king bed.

"I've missed you so much. It seems like we barely get to spend time together anymore between the money making and our family issues," I cried.

"We gon' make it make sense. As soon as I'm where I want us to be in life, we'll have all the time in the world," Jermaine said, kissing my lips.

I couldn't help but unzip his black Polo hoodie, forcing him to take it off as I began kissing his neck down to his navel. Jermaine instantly flipped me over and pulled my plain white T-shirt over my head, revealing my black lace Victoria's Secret push-up bra.

He licked his lips as he undid my bra in the front, placing my nipple into his warm, moist mouth, sending a sensation through my whole body. Jermaine then pulled my panties completely off once he noticed I was in the mood. As he slid his rock-hard penis inside of me, I couldn't help but let out a soft moan.

"Mmmmm, baby, make love to me," I said.

Every time Jermaine and I had sex, it was always rough. Even when he took my virginity, it was rough and hard to enjoy, but I figured because it was my first time, that was why it was painful. This nigga acted like he didn't know how to make love at all. Ignoring what I said completely, Jermaine forced himself inside of me, going harder and harder. He then flipped me on top of him, and I began riding him in slow motion.

"This feels so good, baby," Jermaine moaned

"I know it does, daddy. Mmmmm," I moaned.

Seconds later, Jermaine grabbed me by my hips and began fucking me hard while lying underneath me. I felt my legs go numb as I began to cum. A few seconds after, Jermaine pulled out, and his semen went all over my stomach. He quickly got up and grabbed a towel.

"Sorry, ma. I really didn't mean to do that," Jermaine said. He'd never let himself go inside of me, but he would usually have a towel nearby to release.

"It's OK, baby," I replied, dry as hell.

Don't get me wrong. Jermaine fucked me good, but I really loved him, and I was sure he felt the same, so why couldn't he just show that in the bedroom instead of being so rough all the time? I was annoyed as hell with him. Rolling over, I drifted off to sleep with anger, ready for the next day.

CHAPTER SIX

Porsha

I still couldn't believe Jermaine and Ace had killed Cal together. I had nightmares every night that the Atlanta Police Department would bust down our doors, taking the two men Mookie and I had finally started to love away from us forever; either that, or Mookie getting some information that I knew about this all along. My conscience was eating me alive, but I had to fake the funk.

Jermaine was really changing the person my parents had created me to be. I had started moving weight for him, hiding secrets from my best friend, and now murder. I just couldn't stomach it all.

A FEW MONTHS HAD PASSED, and Mookie was seven months pregnant. She and Ace had gotten close and were even talking about moving in together permanently. I felt like such a bad friend because I was holding so much from her, but at this point, there was no turning back.

Mookie had found out she was having a baby girl, something

she didn't mind having, especially since she was a girly girl. We had all come to the decision that we would move into separate houses because with the baby coming soon, Mookie would need more space, and Jermaine and I needed our privacy. This was my senior year, and there wasn't a need for me to stay on campus, especially when I had business to handle out here with my man. It was the middle of the semester, and I just withdrew from all my classes. My dad was calling me constantly because I was sure the school had notified him of my withdrawal. I just shot him a text and told him that I needed a break, and I promised I would go back. He didn't respond, which was typical of him anyway. We hardly could keep a conversation without arguing. In reality, I didn't plan on it—at least not right now anyway. Money was too good.

Ever since the night it was revealed that Cal's body was found, oddly, that brought Jermaine and me closer together, and we were great as a team. Jermaine was more than a dope seller to me; he was a businessman. I loved a man who was always about their business although I hated that we didn't spend much time together.

Jermaine thought it would be best if we took a trip out of town—him, Ace, Mookie, and me. I had no problem with that, because I did need a break from all the past events that had happened. I loved Atlanta, but I missed my momma even more. Jermaine let Mookie and I pick the place, so, of course, we decided to go to North Carolina and visit our mom.

"Home of the Heels!" I yelled. I was a great fan of our home team, the Tar Heels.

"Damn, it has been a minute since we saw her," Mookie said.

"I mean, honestly, I haven't even talked to her in a while," I said sadly.

My mom and I talked damn near every day, but with everything that had been going on in my new life, I hadn't had time to contact her. I loved my mom to the death of me, and if something happened to her, I would completely lose my mind.

We decided to drive there to make things more interesting, kind of like a road trip.

It didn't take long to get to my mom's, and I thought it would be best to surprise her. Finally arriving at my childhood home, my excitement grew, and I knew my mom would love to see me.

"Look, Mookie. That's the tree where we got caught kissing those boys." I laughed.

"Oh my God, it's still here? Wow, P, we used to be fast as hell," Mookie said.

"No, bitch, *you* used to be fast as hell, influencing me to do stuff I didn't want to," I said jokingly.

Pulling into the driveway, I noticed a car I'd never seen before. Maybe my mom had just bought a new car. She was good for doing things and not telling me until the last minute. It was OK. I'd let her slide this time since we hadn't spoken in forever.

I knocked on the door, but no one answered, which was not normal at my home, so I became worried. My dad's old raggedy, turd green, '96 Ford Expedition wasn't parked out front, but I didn't trip, because maybe my dad had gone to play cards as usual. He was known around High Point for gambling, and if he could, he would put his life on the line. To my surprise, a white man finally answered the door.

I looked at him strangely. "Uh, who are you?" I said.

"My name is Jerry Lewis, and you are?" he asked.

"I'm Nicole's daughter. She lives here," I said, trying to be polite. Who was this white man answering my momma's door? He looked at me with a saddened yet confused face.

"Wow, so you don't know what happened? I'm surprised no one has called you," he said.

"What? Told me what? What are you talking about?" I asked.

"Your mother, Nicole, she passed away. Her high blood pressure caused her to have a sudden stroke that later followed by a severe heart attack. She was on life support for about two months. Your father and I used to work together on the road, and he sold me this home almost immediately after she passed," he said.

I couldn't believe what this man was telling me, but why would he lie? He didn't know me from Eve. I couldn't believe this man. I wanted to know what happened. What led to the heart attack? Why didn't my dad call me? My knees began to buckle as I felt tears forming in my eyes. I fell to the ground, weeping.

"This is all my fault!" I yelled.

I had so many unanswered questions, and I needed to leave.

Jermaine held me in his arms as I cried. My whole world had been crushed. I didn't know what to say or think. The only thing I could think about was getting back to the money for some reason.

That was what Momma would want me to do. Probably not the way I was doing it, but oh well.

After going all the way to NC, happy and ready to see my mom, just to be devastated and at a loss for words sucked! My friends tried to make the best of it for me, but I really wasn't feeling it. However, I really appreciated Jermaine, Ace, and Mookie being there for me; it meant a lot to me. Having my little family by my side completed me. I mean, really, they were all I had at this point.

Jermaine

For some reason, I couldn't stop thinking about the death of my mom. I had never told P. I honestly didn't feel like it was the right time now anyway. I grew up in the streets and considered Ace my brother because his family had adopted me and basically raised me throughout my whole childhood—paying for my food, washing my clothes, motivating me to be better, and putting me through school. They strived for me to be a better person.

Ace's mom was a single parent, but she did a damn good job raising us. She was one of the best lawyers down south, and everyone in the city wanted her to fight their case. My dad died before I even got to know him fully. He was shot in the head during a bad drug exchange. I guess that's where I got my street side from. My mom had died a year after I found my sister, Chelsea. My mom never wanted anything to do with me. Chelsea wanted me to come to her funeral, but I didn't do funerals, and I wasn't ready to see her like that. I regretted not going now. People in school used to tell me how she was a drug addict, but that didn't do shit but make me want to fight anybody who spoke ill of her. I knew my mom was on that shit heavy, but she promised to let it go. She promised me. I used to visit her all the time, but she didn't want to be in my presence unless I was giving her money.

One day I left from school to go check on her and found her in the kitchen, head slung over on the table, foam coming out her mouth, a rubber band wrapped around her arm, and a needle sticking out the thickest vein in her arm. I could never shake that image. I walked the streets day and night, still going to school, sleeping where I had to until I met Ace my freshman year in high school. We became close, and I told him everything. Ever since then, that had been my right-hand man, my brother from another mother. He understood me.

Seeing Porsha break down like that did something to me. When she hurt, I hurt too. I could imagine exactly how she felt right now, and I just wanted to make things right for my girl. I wanted to be there for her as much as possible. While Ace was being there for Mookie, I decided to take Porsha away from the bullshit because it seemed like every time we turned around, something bad happened.

PORSHA

After my mom died, that shit ate me to the core. I went days without eating, and Jermaine had to damn near force me to eat. I just couldn't do it. I was all fucked up, and I knew I would never get over this. All my broken promises to come see her, and the shit had finally come to bite me in the ass. But on some real shit, this had turned me into a savage. I knew my mom wouldn't want me out here doing what I was doing, but fuck it. I had changed for me. I felt like I was in school to be something I wasn't.

CHAPTER SEVEN

Porsha

Months had gone by, and I was back to my usual self. Yes, I missed my mom, but I'd missed my grind as well. With my mom passing and me going through that period of depression, I was more than ready to get back to the normal me. Jermaine had to take over while I was down bad, which he didn't mind, and I didn't either. But I came to the conclusion that it was time for me to suck it up.

I finally spoke with my dad, and that was the most awkward and saddest phone call of my life. My mom had a lot of health issues, but she usually kept it under control. My dad told me he blamed himself because he took her through so much shit.

"She was becoming forgetful because of me. I had started leaving her alone more while I was out with other women. Sometimes I would even tell her I was at work, and I would be right in North Carolina with another woman. I knew she knew, but I didn't know I would be the death of her," my dad cried into the phone.

"It should've been you," I said, disconnecting the call.

I really didn't have shit to say to him. I didn't feel bad at all for him; if anything, I felt bad for my mom for marrying that piece-of-shit ass man. He knew exactly how I would feel about the situation because I had no problem voicing my opinion about the way he treated her when I was younger. I didn't want shit to do with him.

JERMAINE and I were driving around town, making our usual plays, while Mookie and Ace sat at the house, taking care of the new baby, of course.

"I feel like Ace is doing pretty good playing step daddy and shit. What you think, bae?" I joked to Jermaine, and he laughed.

I was trying to lighten the mood since Jermaine was always so tense and hardcore when we were out handling business. In the back seat, we had it loaded with the most potent drug around—that heavy shit called "white girl" and two big ass AK machine guns. We had a connect in the army. I just knew if we were to get pulled over, shit would be hectic as hell.

I didn't want to think about it too much, because too much bad shit had already happened to me at this point in my life, and the last thing I needed was to be behind bars. I asked Jermaine where we were going because it was taking entirely too long to get to this next drop. I was a little skeptical because Jermaine hadn't told me who we were making the drop to. All I knew was that it was some new guys he had recently met up with. I always stressed that Jermaine stay on top of his shit and was sure he stayed on his Ps and Qs when it came to new buyers.

Well... at least I *thought* he had taken my advice, especially with what had happened with Cal.

We pulled up to an abandoned warehouse, and I said, "Jermaine, are you sure about this?" I had a weird feeling in my gut.

"Baby, we good. Just chill," Jermaine said, kissing my forehead.

Walking into the warehouse, I felt the urge to grip my gun. I made sure my gun was on my waist at all times during a drop because things could always go wrong. Jermaine carried the other piece in the back of his pants, and I felt so comfortable and safe with my man. I had nothing to worry about.

Looking around the empty warehouse, I didn't see anything but a bunch of crates.

"Are you sure we're in the correct spot, Jermaine?" I whispered.

"Yes, bae, we are. I'm positive. What did I say in the car? Just chill," Jermaine said.

"Better not be a setup." I rolled my eyes but continued walking, grabbing my gun even tighter, ready to pull it out and shoot. Jermaine walked with so much confidence, carrying two black duffel bags full of drugs. I was so happy to be back to work.

The place was so quiet, almost too quiet, and I couldn't resist hearing our footsteps against the hard, concrete floor. I already had a bad feeling about this, but I shook it off. Jermaine knew what he was doing.

"Freeze! Put your hands up in the air and drop your weapons!" I turned around to see four Atlanta police cars and one SWAT truck.

"Fuck!" Jermaine yelled.

"Bae, oh my God. Oh my God, what should I do? Do I shoot?" I cried.

Something in me wanted Jermaine to say, 'Yeah, baby, start bustin'!' When he didn't, that shit confused the fuck out of me. I couldn't believe we were in this fucked-up situation. I couldn't even think straight. I had just told him how I didn't want this to happen. I hated Jermaine so much for this moment.

Riding in the back of a police car was never what I envisioned for myself, and I immediately regretted giving Jermaine the opportunity to tag along.

Is this what my life is now?

I couldn't believe Jermaine wasn't moving smarter than this. The undercover cops told us they'd been looking for Jermaine for about two years now. They'd been watching him all along.

Sitting in the cold interrogation room, I lightly tapped on the window to get an officer's attention.

"Can I please get my free phone call?" I asked the officer.

"Sure. Make it quick," the officer said.

I'd never been looked at as a criminal, and I had no idea my life could change in the blink of an eye. I picked up the phone and dialed Ace.

Ring! Ring! Ring!

Damn, answer the phone Ace, please. Finally, he picked up.

"Hey, Ace, this is P. Jermaine and I are downtown at the police station. Please come down here and see what's going on. I'll explain all of it to you later," I cried.

"A'ight, sis, give me ten minutes, and I'll be there," Ace said.

I was really thankful for him. He was almost like a brother to me, always making sure I was straight and kept a level head, especially after my mom died. He was around a lot, helping Mookie and me get through it. He was so much more mature than Jermaine; you would think he was older.

ACE

I told Mookie to stay home with the baby because I didn't want her and my child at the police station. I found myself hitting a hundred on the highway, but I needed to see what was up with my brother and sister. Arriving no later than the ten minutes I told P I would be, I went straight to the magistrate's office to see what was going on.

Jermaine had taken all the charges, listing Porsha as a wingman, which I expected him to do anyway. I didn't want my brother going down for some bullshit, so I needed to find a way to work shit out, as usual. I needed more time that I didn't have, so this shit wasn't going to be easy. Jermaine always got himself into shit that I had to save him from, but I didn't mind, because that's what brothers did. I wanted to get my mom involved, but that was just too much, and I didn't want her all in my business like that.

PORSHA

Damnit, where is Ace? Man, I'm ready to go. I don't know how this stupid ass system works, but I'm sure he can just bail me out. Jermaine was in custody, and I saw him sitting in the room across from me. Looking through the little window, he whispered, "I love you, baby. I'm so sorry."

I turned my head and walked back to the cold, hard bench they had me sitting on. I felt tears forming in my eyes that I couldn't control, and they fell from my eyelids like Niagara Falls.

I'm not built for this life, man. Why did I think I could do this?

While he was in processing, I was being questioned about my role in the crime, but I didn't speak. Jermaine had taught me well when it came to shit like this. I knew exactly what to say and how to say it, and if they had given me a polygraph test, I would've passed it.

As mad as I was at Jermaine, I just wanted to be in my baby's arms again, but shit looked bad for him at this point.

"There is no point in us keeping you here when we've already got the main suspect. You're free to go, Ms. Wallace."

The officers politely took the cuffs off my wrist and let me go, and I said nothing.

Leaving downtown without Jermaine by my side felt so unreal. I kept pinching myself as I walked from the police station because it all felt like a dream.

I said nothing to Ace as I climbed into the front seat of the car, and that was when the questions began.

Damn, I thought Ace would let me slide at least until we got back home with Mookie, but I guess I owed him this much for coming to the rescue. I knew I had to explain, but I wasn't feeling myself or the situation anymore. Everything was going downhill, and I felt myself becoming overwhelmed, stressed, and depressed all at the same time. I glared out the window in silence.

"OK, P. I know you hurt, and I know a lot of shit is going through your mind right now, but I need to know exactly what happened," Ace said.

"You right, Ace. This has me fucked up bad. First, my mom, now this. I told Jermaine's hard-headed ass to play his cards right, man, but he never listens," I said with attitude.

"Tell me about it, man. Jermaine is really a hot head. I've been getting him out of shit since we were boys, but that's my brother, so that's what I do," Ace said.

"I'm glad he has someone like you on his team, Ace, I swear to God. Basically, we were set up. Jermaine was going to do a drop to some nigga he'd never met before, and before I knew it, we were in the police car, going downtown, and everything was ceased at the scene and taken in. The cops said they'd been looking for Jermaine for more than two years, so it's a wrap for him," I said as I began crying. Fighting my tears wasn't an option. I hated Jermaine so much right now; any other nigga wouldn't put their bitch in this position. I had become so dependent on him I didn't even have money of my own.

"Ma, we gon' get through this. Jermaine gon' be straight. His first appearance will be on Monday, so we just have to get through the weekend. You can do that for him, right?" Ace asked.

"Yes, of course, I can," I said with a shaky voice. Little did he know, I could do more than get through the weekend without his selfish ass.

I'd hold it down.

CHAPTER EIGHT

Porsha

Life had thrown so much at me, and I didn't know if I was able to cope. I started to feel like I had jumped into some shit I wasn't able to handle, but it was too late to turn back. The whole reason I wanted to do this shit was so I could be closer with Jermaine, but I was starting to realize this wasn't me at all. It felt like everything was going in a downward spiral, and I couldn't get my old life back. I lay in my bed, restlessly thinking of my next move. Jermaine's bond wasn't even set. I knew we had money put up to get him out, so I tried not to press the issue too much. All I hoped was that he had a bond.

ACE, Mookie, and I decided it would be best to ride together. Riding in the back seat of Ace's truck gave me too much time to think. Every song that played on the radio made me think of Jermaine.

"Love Don't Change" began to play through the radio.

"Aye, can y'all love birds change the song, please?" I asked, annoyed.

"Get yo' panties out a bunch, P. Jermaine gon' be good. He's coming home with us today. Soon as the judge says the bond, we are bailing him out," Mookie said.

"But, best, what if shit don't go that way?" I asked. I couldn't help but think about the previous activities that caused us to be where we were today.

"Everything will go as planned," Ace said.

I really appreciated them for being by my side with everything that had been happening. Arriving at the courthouse made me feel so sick. We were scanned like criminals and stripped of our belongings as they searched us.

"I try to avoid this place by any means necessary," Ace said.

"I see why!" I said, grabbing my shit from the security guard who had just patted me down.

"They treat everyone like criminals, don't they!" Mookie spat.

The last time Mookie and I were in a courtroom was when the social service worker signed the rights over to my mom to be Mookie's guardian, a day I would never forget. As we sat in the cold, dull courtroom, listening to the judge give bond motions and drop charge after charge, I began to feel hopeful. When Jermaine approached the screen, I couldn't do anything but cry. I hadn't seen my man since the night this all came about, and looking at him in the orange jumpsuit and orange slippers killed my vibe.

"Look at him; he looks depressed," I said.

"Quiet in *my* courtroom, or I'll have to ask you to leave," the judge said. I rolled my eyes. These motherfuckers were really starting to get under my skin.

Ace, Mookie, and I walked up to the judge, and I sensed this bitch was racist. Not even making eye contact with us, she read Jermaine his rights, and the process began. I took a long, deep breath as the judge reread his current charges aloud. Jermaine was already on probation, so I knew they were going to try to fry his ass. This looked so bad on his behalf. The judge introduced us as his family and support.

I smiled when she asked, "Who are you to the defendant?"

"His girlfriend, Your Honor. Porsha Wallace," I said.

"Do you have anything to say on the defendant's behalf, Ms. Wallace?" she asked.

"Yes, ma'am, I do. I want to begin by telling you and the court that Jermaine isn't a bad person; this was just a minor slip-up. He was in the wrong place at the wrong time. No one really knows him like I do besides the two here with me today, Your Honor," I said with confidence in my voice.

I just knew I sounded dumb as hell. He was already on probation. That should've taught his ass a lesson, but no; he had to go and get set up, being so damn money hungry.

Ace and Mookie stood there, letting me defend my man as I should. I'd never been in this situation before, so I just prayed I was saying all the right things.

"I'll definitely take everything you've told me today into consideration, Ms. Wallace. The two next to you, do they have anything to say on Jermaine's behalf?" she asked.

Ace stepped forward. "My name is Ayden King, and speaking for myself and Monique Grace, we're here to show our support. Also, to add to what Porsha said, Jermaine isn't a bad guy. He just hangs with the wrong crowd at times. But, if you were to set a bail for him today, I would make sure he stays on the right track," Ace said.

The judge smiled a crooked smile, looked me in my face, and said, "Thank you so much for that piece, Ms. Wallace and Mr. King. I'll be setting his bail at six hundred thousand dollars , and once that is paid, he will be released with an ankle bracelet monitor, and he will also have supervised probation this time," she said.

Leaving the courtroom, trying to hold myself up, I felt so numb. I really just wanted to walk away from Jermaine at this point because if he would've just listened to me, all of this could've been avoided. But I knew I couldn't just leave him hanging like that, because he wouldn't do it to me. He really put me in a hard spot. I cried not only happy tears because he had finally been given a bond but also tears of sadness because I didn't know where I was going to get $600,000 from.

Jermaine and I had just started getting our business up, and the shit that happened with the police made us fall behind a lot. Walking out the courtroom, I had the weight of the world on my shoulders, but this was something I had to do, and I would do it. I made a promise to him that I regretted even making. Anything for my man. Time for me to start thinking of a game plan.

CHAPTER NINE

Porsha

A few months had passed, and I began to feel upset with myself. This shit was so depressing. If I had kept my ass in school for law, I could've gone about this the legal way, but I realized sitting around and pouting, wishing on shit I should've done, wasn't getting me anywhere. I had to boss up, so that was exactly what I did. Of course, Ace and Mookie were down to ride no matter what because they knew how I felt for Jermaine. He was my everything. Breaking me from my thoughts, Ace knocked on my bedroom door.

"P, you in there?" Ace asked.

"Where else would I be, nigga?" I asked, laughing. Opening the door, Ace walked in and sat on my bed. "I have some shit set up for later, P," Ace said, smiling.

"Well, whatever it is, I don't even care. You know I'm down for the cause. Whatever to bring the money in," I said. Although I really just wanted to leave all the street shit alone, being arrested for my first time ever was really a wakeup call to me.

"I know you are, P. Jermaine never really had a girl like you on his side before, and I'm thankful. This some shit that me and

Jermaine been had in motion though. We just gotta move differently because Jermaine ain't in the picture right now," Ace said. I understood. I really couldn't complain. I was just ready to get my man home.

Ace told me the details about this dude named Hood who had wanted to do business with him and Jermaine, but he wasn't really known, so they weren't sure if he would bring in business like they did.

I SAT and listened to Ace mack on the phone with the dude to set something up. "Yeah, man, we ready to add you to our team if you still down," Ace said.

"Wow, man, y'all for real? Damn, I been waiting on y'all seems like forever," Hood said.

"Meet me at the spot at nine so we can talk more in person. I'ma have my other business partner with me," Ace said.

Hood was somebody Ace and Jermaine had linked with every now and then when they needed to make big moves. He was from California, and he had his own little shit going on up there. The only reason he hadn't been doing business with Jermaine and Ace was that he didn't really trust anybody outside of their circle.

When we arrived at the spot, which was IHOP, Ace suggested we eat too, but at this time, food was the last thing on my mind. I slid into the small booth with Ace sliding in behind me, and sitting in front of us was Hood.

Damn, he's fine as hell, I thought. He was tall as hell, about six feet four if I wasn't mistaken. I loved my men with height on them. He had long, freshly twisted dreads that past his shoulders, reflecting his warm, light milk chocolate skin.

"Wassup, y'all?" Hood said.

Damn, his voice was even sexier. I felt my pussy get wet just from looking at him. What in the fuck? This was Jermaine's now new business partner, and this was strictly business. What in the hell was I thinking!

"What's good witchu, man? I'm glad you still wanted to take us up on our offer. This is Porsha, the girl I was telling you about over the phone," Ace said.

I smiled. "Hey," I said shyly. For some reason, I was happy that Ace hadn't introduced me as Jermaine's girlfriend.

"Nice to meet you, ma. Ace, so how much are we talking?" Hood asked.

"Six hundred thousand dollars even, bro," Ace said. I knew they were speaking about Jermaine's bond. Hood shot me a look that Ace didn't catch and winked at me, and I smiled back slightly.

"Money ain't nothing, bro. You know that," Hood said.

For some reason, that turned me on so much. I loved a man with money. I wasn't a gold digger, but something about him made me reconsider. I was so used to Jermaine taking care of everything that things just didn't feel the same. I kept trying to shake the thought, but I couldn't. He just really made me feel some type of way.

"So you down?" Ace asked.

"And is," Hood replied.

After sealing the deal, he shook Ace's hand and hugged me tightly. I stepped back, and he looked at my face with his deep-brown eyes as if he were trying to read me. I felt so lost, so I quickly turned around before Ace noticed the interaction. Walking back to the car, I watched as Hood walked to his Chrysler 300, handing Ace the money, and Ace made the exchange.

"Keep us posted on how business goes, bro," Ace said.

Hood made eye contact with me and licked his lips. "Oh, bro, you know I will, no doubt," Hood said, turning to get back in his car. I couldn't help but smile. I didn't understand why Hood was making me feel like this, but fuck it. I just hoped Ace hadn't caught on to any of the childlike flirting back in IHOP. That was the last thing I needed was for something to get back to Jermaine. Snapping out of my thoughts, I began checking my pockets for my phone.

"Damn," I said.

"What's wrong, sis?" Ace said.

"I must've left my phone in there on the table. Hold up while I go get it," I said.

I ran inside, and thankfully, my phone was still under a napkin sitting on the table. I didn't recall leaving it like that, but something told me to pick the napkin up.

On it was Hood's phone number, followed by a little note that read:

Text me, ma.

I felt myself smiling. I was so happy and caught up that I didn't hear the horn blowing outside. It was Ace, so I stuffed the number in my pocket and pushed the thought away before Ace started questioning me. We had both agreed on getting Jermaine out the next morning, and for some reason, I was no longer in a rush. When we returned home, I decided to text Hood. I just wanted to see what he wanted to talk to me about. I lay in my bed, debating if I should even text him. *Fuck it.* I sent him a quick text.

Me: Wassup, Hood? This P.

Hood: Let's get to the point. You're beautiful as hell, and I know you got a man, but I wouldn't mind getting to know you better. Let's meet up tonight before you get him out and see if I can change your mind about some things.

I didn't know what Hood meant when he said he knew I had a man. Maybe Ace had told him, or maybe he was just assuming I had one.

If he tried some funny shit, I would be sure to let Jermaine know everything.

I didn't want to seem too available, but I wrote him a quick message back.

Me: No funny shit OK. I'll meet you, just send me your location.

Damn, how am I going to get past Mookie and Ace? The mutha-fuckas are always on my back, checking for me.

"Hey, Mookie and Ace!" I called from the hallway.

"Yeah, wassup, best?" Mookie said.

"I'm about to go get a drink. I need some time to myself," I said, trying to sound as believable as possible.

"OK, girl. We'll be here when you get back!" Mookie said.

"You need some fresh air anyways, P. You starting to look like a crackhead," Ace said jokingly.

"Ha-ha-ha," I said, repeating his ugly laugh.

I wasn't shocked that she hadn't asked to tag along, because Mookie was a mother now, and she was all about being a family. I was actually proud of her for being a great mother, and I was proud of Ace for stepping up and taking care of Maliyah like she was his own. That took a real man.

I felt overwhelmed about going to meet Hood, but that nigga was fine as hell, and I really couldn't resist. Whatever he wanted to talk about, I didn't mind listening. I really just wanted to get out the house and get some fresh air. I had so much built up inside, and I wanted to release some of that to someone outside of our circle.

HOOD TEXTED ME AN ADDRESS, and I put it in my GPS and followed its instructions. I was so anxious. Once I reached my destination, it was a big ass powder-blue house with a big front yard. I pulled into the long, narrow driveway and texted Hood to let him know I was outside. He told me to walk to the side door, so I did, and he opened the door, wearing a fresh, clean white tee and gray sweats revealing his manhood. Man, he looked good, and I couldn't control myself as I slowly walked up and hugged him. He hugged me back tightly. It felt so good having contact with a man. I knew it hadn't been long since Jermaine had left, but it felt like it had to me.

Hood grabbed my hand, and I walked behind him, looking around, observing my surroundings.

His house was so quiet and clean, unlike Mookie's place where we lived like teenagers. Mookie had baby toys and shoes everywhere. It looked like how my mother would keep her home.

"Don't you think you're a little too old to be living with your mom?" I asked sarcastically.

"I don't live with my damn momma; this my shit," Hood said, laughing off what I had said.

"Well, it damn sure looks like an old head lives here with how neat it is," I said jokingly.

"Oh, hell, don't tell me you don't know how to keep a house clean," Hood said with his lame ass comeback.

I laughed. "Nigga, bye," I said.

This man standing before me was so handsome, and it felt like God had sent him because he and I had an immediate connection. Hood made me feel comfortable around him. He was so free spirited and not street all the time. His vibe was so easy to like. We sat on the couch, and I caught myself staring at him as he played the game.

"Is that what you called me over here for? To watch you play the game?" I laughed.

"You got a slick ass mouth. I like it though," he said, smiling at me sexually.

"I mean, I just keep it blunt. But can I vent to you for a second? I know we barely know each other, but there's a lot on my chest I need to get off, if you don't mind," I said. I really just wanted to talk to someone without being judged. Period.

"Sure, Porsha, I'm all ears. I really ain't here to judge you, ma. Yo' business is yo' business, you feel me?" Hood said.

"Well, I appreciate that, Hood. I just feel like Jermaine and me never really spend time together. He's strictly about the streets, and I feel like I'm losing myself. There's so much going on right now in my life, and I can't control anything. With my mom dying, Jermaine being locked up, and everything falling on me to handle, it's emotionally overwhelming," I cried out as all of my emotions flowed out of me, and it actually felt good to let all of it out.

I didn't want to go too much in depth about how Mookie's mom had overdosed, how my mom was in an abusive relationship, and how I had dropped out of school. That was too much, especially since we had just met.

"I know where you coming from, ma, but I'ma give you my advice on all that. If a man can't appreciate you and spend time with you, then he don't deserve you. On another note, he shouldn't be putting you in the predicament where you feel like you have to change to be accepted by him," Hood said sincerely while still playing the game.

He was right. I didn't deserve that, but it wasn't like he had forced me; I decided to make those moves with him, but he was right. The only reason I made that move was to feel accepted by Jermaine. I began to feel guilty for even telling him after the response he had given me.

He looked over at me as I began to cry. Not just a simple cry either; I was bawling, and the tears wouldn't stop. He paused the game, looked over at me, then pulled me close and kissed me. I kissed him back passionately. What the fuck! What did I just let him do?

I backed away and paused for a second, and he grabbed me again and began kissing me back fiercely, undressing me as I undressed him. I knew this was wrong, but I didn't want it to stop.

Before I knew it, Hood was on top of me, my bra was off, and my breast was in his warm mouth as he played with my nipple with his tongue while grabbing my other one. I softly moaned in his ear as he unbuckled my pants. I pushed him away slightly but not enough to cause him to stop. He kissed me softly then kissed from the crease of my neck to the crease of my other lips. As he went down on me, licking the hurt and anger out of me, I intertwined my fingers in his dreads.

"Hood, oh my God, I'm about to cum, baby," I moaned.

He sped up, French kissing my clit softly, sending me into overdrive. Jermaine did this before but not as good as Hood. He grabbed my thighs as he devoured my pussy.

"Ohhh my God, Hood!" I screamed. I felt myself about to cum, so I attempted to push his head back to warn him, but he didn't stop.

Jermaine's face popped into my head, and guilt took over my body. The satisfaction I'd received wasn't even worth it. It felt good for the moment, but things weren't supposed to go left like they had.

"I should've just stayed home. I should've never texted you," I cried.

"Porsha, it's not that deep. He was selfish enough to put you in a position I never would. I'm stepping in where he can't to satisfy you, ma," Hood said.

He did have a point. Jermaine didn't even give me the benefit of the doubt. He didn't even listen to me when I told him I had a gut feeling. He always left me for hours, sometimes all day, to make plays. Jermaine didn't care about me.

"Well, I love him," I said.

"Come on, Porsha. I know you love him, but he ain't good for you," Hood said.

"Bye, Hood. I gotta go," I said. I quickly jumped up, grabbed my jacket, pulled my pants up, and ran toward the door, but Hood grabbed me before I reached the door.

"I'm sorry, Porsha. I didn't mean to do that," Hood said.

"I'm not some hoe, so don't make me out to be that, Hood," I cried out. I felt so bad for cheating on Jermaine. I had the best nigga around; well, at least that's how I felt.

"I know, Porsha, I know. We both just got caught up in the moment. I said I apologize. You don't say anything, and I won't either."

I couldn't even take him seriously. I wasn't even that type of girl. I snatched away from Hood and ran to my car, crying the whole way home.

Was I going to tell Jermaine what had taken place, or was I going to keep it secret? That was the only thing on my mental. I was already hiding so many secrets from everyone. First, I couldn't trust Jermaine; now I couldn't even trust myself.

I knew for certain Jermaine meant everything to me, and I didn't want him to leave me. We were supposed to have a future together, but what had just happened with Hood had an effect on me, and I didn't want to end it. There was a sexual attraction, and the mouth was intense.

"Fuck my life. I wish I could just call my mom," I cried out. "She would know exactly what to do."

CHAPTER TEN

Porsha

I decided that telling Jermaine wasn't an option at this point. Shit, losing him behind this wasn't an option either. Pulling into Mookie's driveway, I definitely had my heart on my shoulders. I wanted to talk to Mookie about what had happened with Hood but not right now. I just couldn't. Walking into my best friend's house, I smelled baby food and formula. I tried to rush to my room to avoid all conversation, but, of course, that was impossible with Mookie.

"Best, you're back? How was the bar?" Mookie asked me.

"Huh? The bar?" I asked, almost blowing my cover.

"Bitch, you ain't that drunk. You don't remember which bar you went to?" Mookie asked, laughing.

"Oh, girl, my bad. Yeah, my mind just been everywhere. I only bought one drink; that's why I'm back so early," I said.

"Probably because you didn't have your best drinking partna with you," Mookie said, and we both laughed.

"Girl, I'm so tired," I said, trying to avoid conversation.

"Take your ass to bed then," Mookie said, burping baby Maliyah.

I walked into the room, feeling depressed. I thought going to talk to Hood was going to make me feel better, not worse.

Jermaine

Man, I was glad my girl had made something shake. She and Ace never let me down, but I had to move smarter, man. I was being too greedy, but I loved fast money. That shit made my world go around.

I should lay low from the dope game for a little bit to spend more time with my family, I thought. Nah, I couldn't. P loved money too, and if she had a problem with it, she would've told me.

"Jermaine Foster," the CO said.

Finally, damn. "Yes, that's me!" I said.

"It's time for your release. Your family is here," the CO said.

The CO walked me to a small ass room and handed me a box of the stuff I had come in with. Then he allowed me to go into the bathroom to get dressed. Taking the orange jumpsuit off felt so good, and I was ready to be home with my girl. Putting my black Polo sweat suit on with my white high-top Forces brought back the memories of when I got busted a few months ago and had my girl in a messy ass situation. Walking out of the jailhouse, I saw Porsha, Ace, Mookie, and baby Maliyah standing there, waiting for me. It felt good to have a family.

"Let's go eat, y'all. That jail food nasty as hell. Only thing good was the block bread," I said. They all ran up and gave me a hug. Cruising down the highway on the way to IHOP, our favorite restaurant, I was so glad to be home. As we all gathered in the booth, laughing, talking and reminiscing, it actually felt good to be back with my little family once again. I missed them and the bond we had.

Porsha

Later that night, lying in bed with Jermaine, there was really nowhere else I wanted to be. He completed me in so many ways. This man was my whole heart. Although we were young, I knew for a fact this was where I wanted to be forever. Doing something I never usually did, I went down on Jermaine. I didn't know if it was because I felt guilty about the whole situation between Hood and me, but whatever. Waking Jermaine up to my warm, moist mouth would surprise him for sure. I heard him moaning while I was under the covers, deepthroating his manhood. I was surprised at my own actions. Letting Jermaine release himself into my mouth, I swallowed, feeling freaky as ever. I climbed on top of him, bouncing up and down.

"I hope you not trying to make me a dad," he said sarcastically.

I giggled. "No, I can't make you something you already are to me," I said sexily.

Switching positions, Jermaine laid me on my back with my legs tightly wrapped around his back, and he began deep stroking me.

I whispered in his ear, "I love you."

"I love you so much more, P, and I've missed you. I'm sorry," Jermaine said.

After cumming three times, Jermaine and I drifted off to sleep in each other's arms.

WAKING UP THE NEXT MORNING, I knew there was something I needed to figure out. Hood had hit me up the same night I let him eat me like it was his last supper to say he wanted to meet with me again. I didn't return his text, because Jermaine was getting out the next day, but I wanted to take him up on his offer just to end things. How was I going to meet up with Hood without Jermaine knowing? I quickly decided that I would tell Jermaine I was going to visit my dad since he was in town even though I said what I had to say the last time I talked to that nigga on the phone.

"Hey, babe!" I yelled at Jermaine as he took a shower.

"Yeah, ma, wassup?" Jermaine asked.

"My dad called me today, and he wants to meet with me. I feel like this would be good for us. What do you think?" I asked Jermaine, hoping I sounded as believable as I wanted to.

"Hell yeah, baby, go see him. You only get one dad; plus, this will give you the closure you need. I'll be out all day with Ace, making money, so it's cool," Jermaine said.

"OK, daddy, be safe. I'll be here when you get home. Text me if anything goes left," I said.

"A'ight, bae, I love you," Jermaine said.

"Love you too," I said.

Jermaine didn't question what I was telling him, because he knew I wasn't the lying type. I had decided long before Jermaine got out that I would take a break from the trap shit and let him handle it. Deep down, I was ready to get back in grind mode. I felt bad for telling Jermaine that bold ass lie, but I was trying to better our relationship. Between him and Hood, I felt really torn, but I wanted to end it with Hood; at least I thought I did.

Driving to Hood's house, I was happy about seeing him. I honestly believed there was only a lustful connection between us because he was so damn fine. Just thinking about him gave me butterflies. I was determined to let him know this would be his last time seeing me because I was in a full-blown relationship, so whatever he thought we had going on would need to be put to an end quickly.

Arriving at his house, I pulled into the driveway as I did before. Hood was on the porch, smoking a blunt, and when he saw me pulling up, he quickly ran to my door and opened it for me, which took me by surprise. I jumped out of my car, walking with a bounce.

"Happy much?" Hood asked, completely catching me off guard.

"Dude, ain't nobody happy to see your ass. This is just my usual walk," I said, laughing.

"A'ight, whatever you say," Hood said, smiling. I rolled my eyes. Walking into his home, I smelled something cooking.

"What are you trying to cook?" I asked.

"A meal for my lady," Hood said, trying to sound romantic.

"Is your lady in the closet or something?" I asked jokingly.

"Nah, ma, she right there in front of me," Hood said, smirking.

For some reason, that shocked me, but walking into the kitchen behind him, I saw a bottle of Patrón sitting on ice and two wine glasses. I thought, *What's the special occasion?* He pulled my chair out for me, and I sat down. Walking to the stove, he pulled out baked chicken and shrimp alfredo.

"I've never eaten like this before, nor have I been catered to like this, Hood," I said.

He smiled and kept fixing my plate. As we began eating, we talked about random, off-the-wall shit, like schools we went to, our favorite subjects, and where we were before we got to the business we were in now. Hood seemed so interested in me, but I just wasn't up for it. Hood poured me some Patrón, and although I didn't really like this type of liquor, I had some anyway.

What would it hurt?

"Don't try to get me drunk, nigga," I said after taking the drink.

After about three shots, I felt the sober me leaving. "Um, I need to go," I said, damn near slurring my words, but I was sure he had heard what I said.

"I'm not letting you leave drunk, Porsha. Are you dumb?" Hood asked.

"Nigga, you ain't my daddy. My daddy didn't tell me what to do, and neither do yo' ass," I said, slurring even more.

Again, this lying thing was becoming second nature for me. I had just told this nigga he wasn't my daddy and my daddy didn't tell me what to do. Who did I think I was?

"Well, you aren't leaving. Period," Hood said.

"I wasn't g-g-going to leave anyways. Well, at least not right now," I said.

I couldn't even talk correctly. I found myself slurring my words and stuttering, and Hood and I laughed at our actions.

Hood got up and approached me with a soft, wet kiss on my lips. I grabbed him closer, shoving my tongue into his mouth softly. He kissed me back, grabbing my ass through my black sweat suit. I couldn't resist him anymore. I wrapped my arms around his neck, pulling him closer to me; the intensity of him on me made me want him even more. He began undressing me slowly, starting with my pants, revealing my pink lace VS thong. His manhood felt so much bigger than Jermaine's, so he was already winning in my book. Hood had me bent over the kitchen counter before I knew it.

"Mm, your pussy is sooooo wet," Hood said, moaning in my ear.

"I've never felt like this before. Mmmm." I screamed at the top of my lungs. This was the first time a man had ever made me nut in three minutes tops. He had me standing up while he stood straight up inside of me.

"Call me daddy," Hood grunted.

"Daddy!" I moaned as I came all over his manhood.

Hood carried me over to the couch and laid me down then began sucking the soul out of my pearl. My back was arched, and I felt like I was about to do a damn backbend. I couldn't control myself; I came right in his mouth and instantly sobered up.

"Shit! Shit! Shittttt!" I yelled.

Oh my God, what had I just done? I couldn't believe I had just had sex with Hood, and I had just had sex with Jermaine the night before. Neither of us used condoms. I was a hoe. My momma told me about my kind. I cried.

I immediately jumped up and said, "Listen, Hood. This was never supposed to happen. I just wanted to come over here and end things with you. Whatever you thought we had, I didn't mean for it to go this far. I apologize, but I am in a full-blown relationship. I don't want you. I love Jermaine. That's where my heart is," I said, being firm to my word, damn near out of breath, trying to squeeze the long statement out in one breath.

Hood looked at me with a blank ass face as if I were speaking a different language. I didn't care what the fuck he thought, so I grabbed my shit and left. I felt so guilty once again, and the whole ride home, I couldn't even process why I had let it get this far. *The Patrón—that's what did it. I hate that shit!* It was supposed to remain strictly business, but no. I had to fall into his stupid ass trap.

Dumbass bitch, I thought.

Arriving back at home, I made up some bizarre story about how my dad felt so bad for my mom's death and wanted me to come visit him more often, but I just couldn't forgive him for not telling me what happened to my mom when it first happened. All of my lies were starting to pile up, and it became hard for me to keep up with my shit. I wasn't good with this lying stuff. It wasn't for me.

———

HOOD WAS BLOWING my shit up with that 'I want to be with you, Porsha. Why can't you see that?' bullshit, but I wasn't trying to hear any of that. I kept leaving his ass on read and deleting the messages as I went. I didn't even mean for it to go down like that, so why couldn't he just take what I told him and run with it?

I guess Jermaine felt me being distant.

"P, we need to talk, ma," Jermaine said.

"Sure, babe, about what?" I asked. I grew worried. What if he found out what happened? What if Hood got tired of me not replying and told him?

The text messages had stopped between Hood and me, and I just assumed he had given up, which was good. I was ready to forget this all. Jermaine had all his things packed when I walked into the room.

"Uh, babe, what are you doing?" I asked him.

"I'm leaving you, Porsha. I was waiting for you to be honest with me. I thought we were better than that. I already knew you was fucking that nigga, but for you to keep hiding shit from me really hurt me. I'm done," Jermaine said.

My heart stopped. "Wait, what do you mean, you're leaving me? You can't, Jermaine. No, you can't do me like this. After all we've been through, no, please don't go." I found myself begging him to stay with me, but his mind was already made up. Niggas were so quick to call it quits when you fucked up, but when the shoe was on the other foot, they expected you to understand why their nasty asses did what they did.

"Nah, I'm good on all that," Jermaine said.

"Baby, listen. I know what I did was wrong. I told him I had a man, and I cut him off. I want you and only you, nobody else," I said with tears in my eyes.

"If you wanted me and only me, you wouldn't have been fucking some other nigga and lying to me about it. I had to find out from this nigga. You'll figure it out. You was supposed to be my wife, but I guess shit just wasn't meant to be between us," Jermaine said.

I could tell he was hurt, and all I wanted to do was explain myself to him and tell him how sorry I was, but Jermaine wasn't having it. He dragged his shit to the car, explaining to Ace that he was going away for a while. I couldn't believe Hood's snitching ass. What happened to us keeping it a damn secret? When he left, I became so depressed, and I couldn't function. I had stopped eating, and I had lost so much weight. I just wanted my man back. Apparently, Hood had told him what happened between us. This was something I just couldn't cope with. I texted him every day with no reply, but something told me to check my phone, and there was a text from Hood.

Hood: If I can't have you, nobody will. I mean that, ma.

This stupid ass nigga. Having good pussy was definitely a curse.

I swore I could blow his brains out. I didn't want him. What couldn't he get through his head?

Me: Fuck you, bitch.

My feelings weren't as strong for Hood as they were for Jermaine, but he really had me tight right now. I just couldn't believe shit had played out like this. I had really lost my man, but I was going to do whatever it took to win him back!

CHAPTER ELEVEN

Porsha

Jermaine was so damn stubborn. Getting Jermaine to talk to me was the hardest thing I'd ever done in my life. I wanted so badly to ask Ace to set something up, but he already knew something was up because Jermaine didn't just take "trips" without me or all of us.

A FULL MONTH HAD PASSED, and I just wasn't myself. I started to get over the situation, but I missed Jermaine so much. It was crazy how when a dude did some shit to you, they expected you to get over it, but when you did something to them, it was like you killed their mom. As harsh as that may seem, the shit was the truth, and it was really starting to piss me off. I just wanted him back in my life, and he was making this shit difficult as fuck. I forgave his ass when he cheated on me with his ugly ass ex-girlfriend. What if he found someone else already? I spent most of my time thinking about the negatives.

I decided to text Jermaine one last time.

Me: I know what I did was bad. Very bad. Hiding it from you was even worse, but damn, can you at least give me a chance to explain myself?

Jermaine never replied, but I hoped by morning he would.

I woke up with a pillow full of tears the next morning and was surprised to see a text from Jermaine.

Baby: Look, P, I know you fucked up and I've fucked up too, but I'm not trying to lose you or what we've built. You mean the world to me. I want to give you a chance to explain yourself. I love you and you da only girl I want, ma. Shit been hard without you.

Reading that text, I was so excited. I didn't know which emotion to feel. I couldn't believe he had made me wait this long to make things right between us. What the fuck?

I quickly replied without hesitation.

Me: Well, hey, thank you for trying. Let's set something up for us to do tonight. I want to redeem myself with you and become your girl again as quick as possible. Babe, I love you so much more. I can't apologize enough for what I've done, but let's meet up tonight at Red Lobster and talk.

Waiting for him to reply, I began thinking about what I should wear tonight. I was so happy he wanted to fix us. I loved this man so much.

As soon as I heard my phone go off, I quickly grabbed it.

Jermaine: I love you too, baby girl. How about something simpler? Just come to the room I've been staying in, and we can stay here a few nights, then go back home together. Don't worry about packing any clothes, I'll take you shopping.

Shopping? Few nights away? Just us? Had he done something wrong? I was completely confused. I mean, I agreed because I wanted to see him, and it didn't matter if it was at a fancy restaurant or a motel.

———

THAT NIGHT, I dressed in a matching royal-blue VS panty and bra set, blue Levi skinny jeans, a mock neck sweater from Forever 21, black knee-high boots, and a freshly shaved cat. Just in case Jermaine felt generous tonight, I was prepared for anything. I looked in the mirror as the thirty-inch Malaysian hair fell to my ass. I had made sure to damn near super glue the lace on my frontal down to make it look natural. I was feeling myself and determined to win my man back. I couldn't wait to see what tonight had in store for us.

Pulling up to the room, I felt embarrassed for how I had done Jermaine. He had done me wrong at the beginning of our relationship, but two wrongs didn't make a right. Entering the room, I saw Jermaine had rose petals all over the bed and a bubble bath with rose petals wrapping around the tub. The room was completely dark, but there were enough candles lit so I could admire the setup.

"Babe, get undressed. We're going to take a hot bath, relax, and talk about us and our future together," Jermaine said. Doing as told, I got undressed and joined him in the bathtub. I looked at Jermaine, and he looked different; his eyes weren't as happy as they used to be. I instantly began to cry.

I really broke this man. How could I do this? I thought.

"Jermaine, listen, baby. I'm sorry for all the pain and hurt I've put you through this past month. I want to explain to you in detail about everything that happened that night and leading up to the night we broke up. I know what I did was completely wrong, and there aren't enough apologies. All I can say is we can start from scratch and put this behind us. I promise you this will never happen again," I cried out.

Jermaine began to tear up as I explained everything to him, not leaving a single detail out, which I should've done from jump.

"I just can't fathom you and him having sex. This nigga slapped hands with me, got my number, and called me his bro, but the whole time, he was trying to get at my girl. I wish this shit would've never happened, because now I got to handle him," Jermaine said.

I knew he was serious. I didn't want him doing anything crazy to risk him any more jail time, but Jermaine was a man of his word. Another part of me didn't want Hood dead either.

After our bath, we lay in the king-size bed, watching our favorite show, Law & Order, and began reminiscing.

"I missed you so much, man," Jermaine said sincerely.

"The feelings are completely mutual, baby." I was so happy I finally had my man back, and this time, I wasn't losing him again.

CHAPTER TWELVE

Porsha

I hadn't heard from Hood in a little over a month, so hopefully, he had finally gotten over himself. I loved Jermaine so much, and I just wanted to be happy with him. Things were finally going how we had planned them in the very beginning. My little family was finally back to normal, and we had no room for any extras... except for our baby boy or girl.

When I first found out, I couldn't believe it.

"Take the test, P," Jermaine said.

"No, Jermaine, I'm scared. I don't even think I'm pregnant," I said, trying to avoid the test.

"Baby, this is all we need to complete our family. We talk about this every day. Just take it, baby, please," Jermaine begged.

"Give me the damn test because you 'bout to piss me off," I said, my mood changing. After waiting five minutes, I found out I was exactly six weeks pregnant. "Wow, I can't believe this shit. Look, Jermaine," I said, handing the test to Jermaine.

"I told you, you were pregnant!" Jermaine said, excited as hell.

FINDING out I was pregnant had me a little worried, but I was so excited, and so was Jermaine. It made me feel even better about this being my first pregnancy.

Jermaine had always been a hot head, and either Ace or I would have to save him, but now, he had a reason to think twice before reacting. It had been nice to see him grow into the man I wanted him to be, and he had improved dramatically. He was still in the drug game but only part-time since Taedoe had stepped in to handle business. Not only that, but he and Ace made it a point to interact with Maliyah and take her out, so I knew he would make a great father.

JERMAINE

Riding around town with six-month-old Maliyah and watching Ace in action with his daughter made me want my child with Porsha even more. We'd been through our ups and downs, but that was my baby. I was just glad we were past all that cheating shit. It still crossed my mind but not as much. Now that we had a baby on the way, it was only up from here.

"Jermaine," Ace said, breaking the silence.

"Yo," I said, kind of mad because he had interrupted my thoughts.

"You ready to be a dad, man? I'm so happy for you. This is exactly what you needed to keep your head on straight," Ace said.

"Yeah, bro, I'm more than ready. When she handed me that test, it just confirmed everything for me, bro. Seeing you out with Maliyah, even though she's not yours, motivates me, bro," I said.

"I ain't tryna sound soft, bro, but this shit so rewarding. This *my* little girl," Ace said.

"Can't wait 'til I can say that. Boy or girl, I'll be fine with a little me," I said. We both laughed because we knew for a fact the streets weren't ready for another me.

Porsha

Sitting in the chair while the nail tech massaged my feet, I decided to let Mookie know what had been on my mind the whole time.

"Best, I gotta tell you something, but this is an actual secret. Like, you can't even tell Ace. You need to promise me you won't," I said, serious as hell.

Just the thought of Hood and me having sex around the same time I became pregnant made me feel sick to my stomach. I wasn't 100 percent sure if Jermaine was the father or not, and the last thing I needed was to damage my family even more. Mookie, Ace, and Jermaine were the only family I had, and this one mistake could ruin everything.

Mookie looked at me with a frown. "You know I don't like keeping secrets. I'm not good at that bullshit, but I'll try for you," Mookie said.

I knew exactly what she meant. She wasn't the type to keep things to herself, but I needed her to promise me on this one. She was the only person I could turn to at this time.

"Just promise me, Mookie, damn," I said, annoyed.

"I got you, man. I promise," Mookie said.

"Well, you know the whole situation with Hood, Jermaine, and myself," I said.

"Yes, P, duh, I know. Don't tell me that nigga getting on your nerves again 'cause we can get him handled," Mookie said, rolling her eyes.

"No, that's not the case. I'm six weeks pregnant, and around that time, me and Hood had sex without a condom. I was caught up in the moment," I said, nearly crying. Mookie looked at me as if I had spoken a foreign language.

"Say whaaat!" Mookie screamed.

"Bitch, oh my God! I knew I shouldn't have said anything; you always doing the most," I said.

"OK, P, you act like this situation is something that can just be overlooked. I'm sure if it is Hood's child, he would want to be in his or her life just as much as Jermaine would want to be if it was his. So what you gon' do?" Mookie asked.

I couldn't even answer her, because I didn't have an answer myself. This shit was tough. I couldn't believe I had let things get that far. I should've just left it at business only, but no. I had to let this nigga get all in my business by letting my emotions and sexual attraction for this nigga consume me. I felt like an idiot.

I wished there were a way to find out who was the dad without them having to know. I immediately went into thinking mode. Maybe I could link up with Hood when it was time for the baby to be born and swab his and Jermaine's mouths, then... Man, none of this shit made sense. I just wanted to go back in time and call my mom; she would've known exactly what to say.

I started getting emotional but was instantly snapped out of my thoughts when the nail tech asked me what color I wanted on my toenails.

"Blue, please," I replied. I smiled at the thought because that was Jermaine's favorite color.

I tried to push those thoughts to the back of my mind because I needed to focus on what I was going to do. I was content with how things currently were. Mookie was the only person who knew, and I liked it that way. Maybe I could avoid telling Jermaine and Hood and just do things my way, but every time I tried to do things my way, things went left.

Checking my phone, I saw a text from Hood.

Hood: I haven't forgotten about you, beautiful. Just wanted to give you your space. Let's go half on a baby.

What the fuck?

He really wanted a baby with me? I thought he had moved on or some shit. Although I was angry, the message made me smile. He had hit me up right in time because I needed to get to the bottom of things. I knew I wasn't going to find out who the daddy was right then and there, but speaking with Hood would finally give him some closure. Hopefully I could keep my pants on. Every time I got around him, I couldn't control myself it seemed like. I quickly shot him a text back.

Me: Nigga, we need to talk. After we talk, I want you to stop hitting my line, for real this time. If you still hmu, I'ma tell my nigga.

I knew I was fronting though. I was definitely trying to play hard to get. I wanted to be in his presence. I just loved the feeling of him fighting for a spot in my life. He was such a nice guy, and he was there for me when Jermaine was locked up.

Two minutes later, he replied.

Hood: Whatever, ma. Where you at? I'll come pick you up if you ain't around yo' "man."

This man really couldn't take no for an answer, and for some odd reason, that suddenly aroused me in many ways than just one.

CHAPTER THIRTEEN

Porsha

After the nail salon, I decided to have Mookie cover for me because I needed to see Hood. Well, I didn't need to, but I wanted to. Something in me told me to go see him.

My best friend, who stood on the other side of the nail salon, yelled, "P, what color should I get, bitch!"

"Pink since that's your favorite color," I replied, rolling my eyes. "Mookie, do me a favor. Pretty, pretty, please," I pleaded, gesturing for her to come a little closer to me so nobody would hear our conversation.

"Hell no! I'm not telling Jermaine that ain't his baby!" Mookie damn near screamed.

"Bitch, that wasn't what I was going to ask you. Just cover for me for a little bit. I'm going to leave and go meet Hood, and I want you to make up a lie," I said.

"A lie? Bitch, a lie? I can't lie, and you know that. What am I supposed to say? You know I don't like being involved in your shit," Mookie said.

She was right. I knew she couldn't lie for shit, but I needed her more than ever right now. Maybe what I was doing was wrong, but maybe if I gave him some closure, he would leave me alone.

"Mookie, just tell Jermaine and Ace I went out to get some things for the romantic dinner I had planned for us tonight," I said, and Mookie rolled her eyes. "You know every time I get in the kitchen, you are down to eat, so don't play," I said. I knew I had won her over with that one.

"A'ight, P, make it quick because I can't lie for long. You lucky you're my bitch," Mookie said. I paid for my pedicure and hers and was ready to go.

Me: Hood, you're aggy as fuck but I want to see you so can you pick me up at the corner of 3rd Avenue? NOW!

I sent it quickly, expecting a fast reply, as usual.

Hood: Good thing you hit me up. I was already on that side of town, dropping off some work to one of my plays.

Smiling at his text message, I caught myself and instantly and made a stern face. Although Hood was such a sweet guy, he wasn't who I really wanted to be with, but him making time for me was something I liked so much about keeping him around. When Jermaine wasn't around, Hood always was even when I didn't want him to be. I thought I was so over this dude until I could no longer contain my smile when I noticed Hood's car, Black Knight as he called it, a mile away.

I jumped in the car quickly, trying not to be noticed by anyone, and a sense of urgency came over me. I looked at Hood, who still looked good as ever. I didn't know what I was expecting since it had only been a few weeks, but damn, he looked even better than I'd left him.

I licked my lips, and he noticed my gesture and took it upon himself to grab me and kiss me before we pulled off. This felt so right even though it was so wrong.

"You know, that was some lame, hoe shit you pulled a while back, ma," Hood said.

I rolled my eyes. "Boy, I had to do what I had to do. I really don't even know why I'm with you right now, to be honest," I said.

"Because you wanna be," Hood said, smiling hard as hell, revealing his pearly whites.

I couldn't stand his ass, but pulling up to his house where we'd last had an encounter brought back so many memories. I was only six weeks pregnant, and you could barely tell, so I decided that would be the last thing I mentioned to him.

As I walked into the house behind Hood, he grabbed my hand as if he were showing me around like I'd never been there. He took me up the stairs to his bedroom and, for some reason, I didn't reject as bad as I wanted to. I knew this was wrong, but I wanted him more than ever. Maybe it was just the pregnancy hormones, but I wasn't going to stop it. He laid me on his bed, pulling my pants down slowly while kissing me.

"Hood..." I tried stopping him.

"I love you, ma. I don't ever want to lose you," Hood said.

I cried softly. I had feelings for two men and didn't know what to do.

Hood was so different. He didn't fuck me rough and fast like Jermaine; he made passionate love to me, and he was so much more mature in bed. He made time for me, and he made me feel like I was the only girl in the world.

Lying in his bed hours later, I felt so guilty. I didn't want to leave, because this seemed like my happy place, the only place I was able to get away from all the bullshit in my life. So many thoughts ran through my head as I rolled over in Hood's arms. He looked into my eyes, and they began to water.

"Hood, I'm pregnant," I said.

He stared at me blankly then instantly got excited. "For real? You pregnant, ma? I'm going to be a dad? I've been waiting for this, man. We would be the perfect family," Hood said with so much excitement.

I must've looked at him like he was stupid because he quickly became defensive. I explained to him how I had been having sex with him and Jermaine around the same time.

"It isn't OK. I'm admitting this to you because you're a lot more understanding than Jermaine is; I just haven't had the guts to tell Jermaine everything. The timing is so wrong," I cried.

"So you mean to tell me that it's OK for you to come to me about some shit and not tell him the whole story? What the fuck, Porsha? I love you, yo, but this shit ain't right, ma," Hood said. I could tell by now he was angry.

"I was going to tell him, just not now. I feel more comfortable opening up to you than him. I've known him longer, but you get me," I said, defensive as hell.

Listen to me trying to make it sound OK to be a hoe and sleep with two men at the same time. Ugh.

Before I knew it, Hood jumped up, grabbed his phone, and was on the phone telling Jermaine everything. "Yo, Jermaine, I know you don't fuck with me, man, but I don't really give a fuck. We have a problem," Hood said to Jermaine. Hood had walked into his master bathroom, and though he had Jermaine on speakerphone, the sound was muffled.

I couldn't move. I had no more fight in me. I had no control of my life, once again, and everything was crumbling around me. I knew this wasn't the right way to tell Jermaine, but I couldn't do it alone. My heart couldn't bear it. Hood walked back into the room, looking at me with an expression I couldn't read.

"I can't believe you, man," Hood said.

"I'm sorry, Hood. I told you this shit shouldn't have happened between us in the first damn place. You knew I had a fucking boyfriend," I said.

"You know what? It wasn't supposed to happen, but it did. You let the shit happen. I didn't hold a gun to your head; you wanted me just as bad as I wanted you," Hood said, extremely upset.

He'd never raised his voice at me before, but I couldn't even fake the funk; this nigga was turning me on.

I walked up to Hood and kissed him gently on the lips. Hood being angry with me was another turn on I couldn't help myself from falling back from.

"Baby, I'm sorry. I didn't mean to hurt you," I said, kissing Hood again.

"P, that shit hurts. I've never been in a situation like this before, yo. I've never felt for a bitch like I feel for you," Hood said, kissing me back.

"You really, really feeling me, Hood? I thought it was strictly sex," I said.

"No one ever stated it was strictly sex, so why would you assume that? It's my fault for getting involved with you and letting it get as far as sex. I fell for you, man. I knew it was a stupid ass move," Hood said.

"It wasn't dumb, and you aren't dumb. Your feelings are your feelings, and you can't help how you feel about someone," I said. Hood grabbed me and pulled me in close, holding me tight.

"Porsha, baby, we'll get through this. We have to. Just know I'm here by your side regardless," Hood said, sounding sincere. I didn't even want to go home. I couldn't face all the shit that had just blown up in my face.

I felt like my whole world was falling apart. I had two great men in my life, and I had fucked everything up. I didn't know what to do, and at this point, I wanted to hide under a rock forever. Jermaine wouldn't want anything else to do with me now that there was a third party involved—my baby. I knew that for a fact after how quickly he had left me when he first found out about Hood. It saddened me because Hood would probably walk away too. Although he said he would stick around, who wanted to raise someone else's baby? God didn't make them like Ace anymore. He was rare as hell, and now I would be left with no one, but I deserved this, I guess.

CHAPTER FOURTEEN

Jermaine

I couldn't believe this bitch. I had given her everything and had made her into who she was today, and she played me? How could she do this? I'd been with this girl since her freshman year in college. How could she let some new nigga fuck her that easily? I decided to call my ex, especially since I hadn't heard from P in over an hour. Myasia might have been a hoe when we were together, but she was always there for me whenever I needed her.

"Hello?" answered Myasia.

"Wassup, ma? This Jermaine. You should recognize this voice," I flirted.

"J, I'm not fucking you, bye," Myasia spat.

"Man, I'm not even with all that. I just wanna vent, man," I said.

"Vent to your ugly ass girlfriend," Myasia said.

"Chill, ma. It don't even gotta be all that," I said. I loved that aggressive shit. She was so demanding, and it was turning me on.

"Ughhh, come over, babe. I'll listen to your sad ass," Myasia said.

"On my way," I said.

On my way to Myasia's house, I was really on the fence about seeing her ass because I knew how it was when we got together. Pulling into Myasia's narrow ass driveway, I was disgusted. Her house looked like no one gave a fuck about the place. Her grass was damn near up to my ankles, and one of the shutters on her windows was damn near on its last leg.

When I walked up to the door, before I could knock, Myasia opened the door with skin-tight leggings on. I could damn near see her pussy print, and her crop top revealed her nipples. I instantly felt myself getting hard, but I quickly jumped back to reality; I wasn't here for all that.

"What's up, daddy? What you wanna talk about?" Myasia asked, guiding me inside.

Even though her house looked horrible from outside, her shit was laid out inside. Myasia had always been extra, so it wasn't a surprise that she had blown-up pictures of herself all over the place. Her living room was nicely decorated with an all-black plush leather couch and a sixty-inch flat screen Samsung smart TV. Myasia wasn't the type to have a game system though, so I was confused about why she had one.

"I hope you don't have another nigga living here since you gave me the OK to come over," I said.

"Nigga, now you know I have a little brother. I got him this shit for when he comes over so he won't be all in my business," Myasia said.

"My fault, ma. I wasn't mad or nothing, I just didn't know you still kicked it with your little brother," I said.

Myasia's family had basically abandoned her when she first started fucking with me a few years back. At first, they acted like they didn't even want her around her little brother, but eventually, I guess they came around.

"Whatever, nigga. I know you miss this pussy," Myasia said sarcastically.

"Nah, not even, but I got some deep shit going on, and I feel like you really the only person I can come to about this," I said.

"Like what, J?" Myasia asked.

"P cheated on me when I was locked up. She had sex with the nigga and me around the same time, and now she's three months pregnant. We've gotten over the cheating part, but this was before we even knew a baby was involved. Now this nigga calling my line like it might be his baby too," I said with anger and sadness in my voice.

Myasia could always tell when I was hurt, so she came up and gave me a hug without speaking. She quickly pulled away. "So, you mean to tell me you left me for a bitch who can't even keep her legs closed?" Myasia spat.

"Ma, now you know it ain't even like that. Porsha is different," I said in her defense.

"Nah, J, not really. But I mean, you like bitches like that. You don't need nobody like that in yo' life; you need somebody who understands you and someone who gets you, like me," Myasia said, leaning in to kiss me.

This girl was really crazy. I didn't even want her after the rumor that was going around town that she tried to sleep with my brother, Ace, then blamed it on the liquor. I hadn't looked at her the same since. Ace never confirmed it, but he didn't need too. I knew what her ass was capable of. I backed up. "Nah, Myasia. I love P. She gets me. She's just trying to find herself, and that shit stressing me and her out," I said in her defense. I could see Myasia getting upset.

"Jermaine, do you really think a bitch is trying to find herself when she out here fucking your business partna? Boy, bye! I knew you was dumb but not this dumb," Myasia said.

She was right. Shit like that didn't just happen.

Before I knew it, I grabbed Myasia, kissing her big, pink, soft lips off instinct and my anger toward Porsha. Myasia was a redbone with soft, long, curly hair. Her mom was white, and her dad was black. She had a nice, full ass that she didn't mind showing off, and her high cheekbones complemented her green eyes. Myasia was fine as hell, but I couldn't trust this bitch. She was completely different from P though. I didn't have to teach her the ropes of the game, because she already knew.

"Mm, J, I've missed you," Myasia said, putting my hand inside of her tights so I could feel her freshly shaved pussy.

"I've missed you too, My," I said, massaging her clit with my fingers. I knew just what Myasia liked. Leading her over to the couch, I continued kissing her as she unbuckled my True Religion jeans. Pulling her shirt over her head, I followed her lead. I loved that she was so aggressive.

"Fuck me, J. You know you want to," Myasia said seductively.

I pulled my dick out and bent her over her black, plush couch. I was already standing at attention, and I could see Myasia's juices dripping down her leg. I stuck the tip in slowly then forced myself inside of her.

"Mmmm, babyyyyy, go deeper!" Myasia moaned.

"You love this dick, don't you?" I asked.

"Yes, daddy! Yesss!" Myasia screamed. I pulled her hair while speeding up my pace, going in and out of her wet, warm cat.

"Mmmm, talk to me, baby," I moaned.

"Don't stop, daddy. Go faster. I'm about to cum all over that dick. Fuck me!" Myasia screamed.

"What the fuck!" I yelled, releasing inside of her, not regretting it at the moment. Myasia didn't care since she had told me she was on birth control.

I lay there with her. Myasia had some good ass pussy, and I really wasn't into giving that up, but sometimes things needed to be that way. She was all right to fuck on every now and then, but she wasn't Porsha. I was holding her in my arms, wishing it was Porsha. I couldn't keep my mind off her. I decided I would let Myasia fall asleep then get my shit and go. This wasn't right; I was just caught up in the moment. Porsha was who I wanted to be with. The heart wants what the heart wants, and I couldn't fight that. Once Myasia drifted off to sleep, I quickly put my clothes on and left.

Driving down the highway, I was ready to get back home to see if

Porsha was there so we could talk face to face. I just hoped like hell she was home. Instantly, I regretted going to Myasia's house, and I knew I would have to explain that to Porsha. We needed to get everything off our chests and leave the secrets in the past. I felt like we were acting like kids, avoiding our problems.

Arriving at Mookie's house, I didn't see Porsha's car parked out front, and that shit really fucked with me. I just wanted to be with my girl, and she was out doing her. I'd never been the type of sucker nigga to chase after bitches, and she was about to make me say fuck her and move on. She was playing too many mind games now.

Me: Porsha, we need to talk, man. I'm not with all this ducking and dodging bullshit you on.

I waited for her response, but instead, a message from Myasia came in.

Myasia: J, you didn't have to leave. Stop treating me like some hoe. You know we are meant to be. Can we link tomorrow? Lunch or something?

I didn't even want to reply; Porsha was the only girl on my mind. Myasia might be the one who was supposed to be my wife. Somehow, we always found our way back to each other, and I was out here chasing Porsha's ass like a fiend.

CHAPTER FIFTEEN

Porsha

I couldn't keep sitting at Hood's house. Although it felt good being in his presence, my heart wasn't there. Jermaine was my one and only. Seeing my phone flash with a notification from Jermaine made me feel a bit of relief. He wanted to talk about everything, and I was down, just not tonight. I was too embarrassed, so I texted him back.

Me: I want to talk about everything and get everything off my chest, but not tonight, Jermaine. I know I owe that to you, but I'm not ready tonight. I'll have a room at Red Roof, and I'll text you in the morning when I'm ready to see you.

JERMAINE

I didn't even want to reply, because my head was racing. How would I explain this to her, and how would she explain the situation with Hood to me? What if she didn't even fuck Hood last night, and I had just messed up any hope for us? I wanted to kill that nigga Hood for even trying Porsha, but who was really at fault? Her or Me? Or were we both equal in this love affair? I didn't care who was right and who was wrong; I just wanted to be with Porsha and Porsha only.

Damn, when did I become a sucker?

Porsha

Driving to the motel, I felt a sense of relief now that I was alone. Maybe that was what I needed from the beginning instead of trying to have a man fill the void.

Once I got to my room, I decided it would be best to take a hot shower. I felt disgusting. I'd never seen myself as a woman who slept with more than one man. I guess this was what Momma meant when she said, *"Life isn't always a walk in the park."* I sure did miss my momma, and I hadn't been to her gravesite since Dad told me where she was buried. Maybe I would make that a priority once I had the baby so he or she could meet Momma. My momma always told me if I were to ever have kids, they couldn't call her grandma; they were only allowed to call her Glam-ma or Rose. I didn't know why she had picked the name Rose, because that wasn't her name or anything close to it.

I walked into the nicely made room. They always left these small ass towels and soap that was barely enough for one shower. I hated motels, but I didn't want to go back home to everyone questioning me about my whereabouts and why I had done what I did. I really didn't have time to explain my business to everyone.

Climbing into the shower, I felt my body relax as the hot, steaming water ran down my back. I let my weave out from underneath the cheap ass plastic shower cap they'd supplied. The water felt so good running through my braids underneath my sew-in.

After my shower, I climbed into the big king-sized bed I'd requested and lay down, fully naked. I thought about the encounter I'd had earlier with Hood when he told me he had feelings for me and was going to be there regardless. I smiled. It was nearly 4 a.m., but I decided to call my best friend. I wanted to apologize for putting her in a difficult position. She didn't deserve that.

"Hey, Mookie," I said, hoping she wasn't upset.

"Best, what the fuck going on? I'm getting dressed right now. Where you at? Who were you with? Wassup?" Mookie asked with urgency.

"Bitch, calm down. I didn't mean to scare you. I know it's late. I just wanted to apologize for putting you in that shit earlier with Jermaine and Hood. I shouldn't have done that," I said with sincerity.

"Don't scare me like that, Porsha. Are you slow? You're my bitch, and I'm always gon' be here for you. We made a promise to each other, right or wrong," Mookie said.

"That's why I love you, girl. I just felt bad for what I did because I wouldn't want to be in a situation that deep. But for you, of course, I would always understand," I said.

"Well, I understand, mama, but you know we ride for each other. I love you too," Mookie said.

"A'ight, well, I'll let you get back to sleep. I know it's late," I said.

"Best, this is my new sleep schedule since the baby keeps me up. But I'll let you go," Mookie said.

"Bye, girl," I said before ending the call with a laugh.

Lying in bed, I kept thinking about Hood and how he'd told me he loved me. I felt like I wanted to make things right with Jermaine, but Hood was my type of nigga—street but respectful. Jermaine, on the other hand, always left me alone at home when he was out handling business. He demanded respect, and he always got it. Plus, he knew his shit when it came to the streets. They were both hood niggas, just two different types.

This was exactly why my dumbass was stuck now. I kept comparing, and they were both amazing. I needed to follow my heart, but I was thinking so much that I couldn't hear my heart. Looking at my phone, I saw it was 6 a.m. Finally feeling at peace, I drifted off to sleep

---

I ended up sleeping later than usual, but I guess that was because I was in my first trimester. I got up and washed my face, then I decided to text Jermaine my room number.

Me: 126. Hurry up.

When Jermaine arrived, I didn't know how to feel, but there were a lot of emotions in the air.

"Wassup, ma?" Jermaine said.

"Hey, Jermaine," I said plainly.

"Let's just get to the point, man. I forgave you for cheating, and I'm sure we can get past this. I feel like I want to be with you and only you, so nothing should hold us back from that, right?" Jermaine asked.

"Jermaine, I didn't mean for it to happen the way it did, I swear.

I'm hoping we can move past this too. I love you, but if we're going to be together, things need to change," I said.

"Noted. I love you too," Jermaine said, kissing me. I didn't push him away, but I didn't want to have sex with him.

"Let's lay down," I said, guiding him to the bed.

"OK, ma, whatever you want," Jermaine said.

We laid down and Jermaine held me and rubbed my stomach. I laughed a little at the thought of having a baby. Lying there in Jermaine's arms made me feel so complete, and I found myself drifting off again.

JERMAINE

As I lay there with Porsha in my arms, I couldn't help but think about the night before when Myasia and I had sex. It was really just revenge sex, but I didn't know how to explain that to Porsha without her leaving for good, so I decided that not telling her would be best. I hated lying, and I did want everything out in the open, but losing her again was not an option.

I wanted some advice on the situation, so I decided to call my brother, Ace. He never failed me when it came to this life shit.

"Aye, bro, I need to talk to you," I said.

"Hold up, bro. Let me step outside," Ace said. "OK, bro, I'm back. What's good with you?" Ace asked.

"Man, look. I did some crazy shit with Myasia, and I don't know how to tell Porsha, man," I whispered.

"Whoa, what the fuck, J! Man, you for real right now?" Ace asked, shocked as hell.

"Yes, man. I know I fucked up bad. I know that, but there's more. I nutted in her, bruh," I said, whispering into the phone.

"J, you gotta tell P, man. The longer you wait, the more it'll affect her once she finds out," Ace said, being honest.

"You right, bro. A'ight, I'ma let you go. I'ma handle this," I said.

Hanging up, I took what Ace said into consideration. He was always right, but I still didn't want to tell her. I couldn't handle it if she left me, but I promised myself I would tell her later. I climbed back in bed and pulled my girl close to me. I sure as hell loved her and our baby. I was determined to not let anything get between us, and I meant that.

Porsha

Waking up from my mini cat nap, I felt so refreshed. I couldn't believe I had stayed up so late the night before, thinking about everything I'd been through over the past few months. It felt good to finally have everything out in the open with Jermaine. I loved how content and honest our relationship was growing to be. I just wanted Jermaine to understand that I wanted him to spend more time with me, and now that we had a baby on the way, he would need to let that street shit go.

"Jermaine, baby," I said.

"Yeah, ma, wassup?" Jermaine asked, sounding concerned.

"Baby, I just want to have a serious talk with you about the real reason for my encounter with Hood. You probably won't believe me, but I want you to hear me out," I said.

"Nah, baby, I'm here to hear you out. I want us to move past this bullshit, ma. I'm all ears," Jermaine said, sounding nicer than usual.

"OK, good, babe. Well, the real reason I was even attracted to Hood was because he did things differently than you. He made love to me, and he made it his duty to make time for me even when I didn't want the shit. I love you, and I don't want you to think I'm saying everything is bad when I'm with you, because it's not," I said.

"I understand, ma. I just be busy," Jermaine said.

"But that's what you don't understand. Us not spending enough time together is pushing me into somebody else's arms, baby. You told me you wanted a ride-or-die chick, and I changed for you. I'm just asking that you make time for me, Jermaine," I cried out.

He pulled me closer to him, and I saw the sincerity in his eyes.

"I really care about you, baby, and I damn sure don't want you to feel the need to be with another nigga. I'ma lay this street shit down for a little bit and take care of home. I love you, baby girl," Jermaine said.

"I love you too, baby, and I sure hope you mean that, Jermaine. I'm tired of feeling alone in this relationship," I said.

"And I don't want you to, ma, so I'ma get my shit together. Matter of fact, I'm about to go handle some shit and let niggas know I'm 'bout to sit down for a little. Do you mind meeting me back at the house in a couple of hours?" Jermaine said.

"Yes, baby, I will. I'm going to get Mookie to go shopping, and we'll be home before dinner," I said.

"OK, bae, that works," Jermaine said.

I called Mookie and let her know that I would be coming to pick her and Maliyah up soon so we could go shopping, and she agreed. I needed to go home and get dressed anyway.

The conversation with Jermaine made me feel secure. I just hoped this nigga was really up to what he said he was and keeping his word. Going shopping with Mookie was really what I needed at the time anyway.

CHAPTER SIXTEEN

Porsha

A few weeks had passed, and going out with my best friend was really what I needed to get positive energy around me. I was so worried about this shit with Jermaine and Hood, and I couldn't think straight. Mookie sounded excited about getting out the house, but I knew she just wanted to hear about my hoe stories.

Walking into my best friend's house, I felt a sense of relief being back home. Since I had taken a shower early this morning, I ran to my room to get dressed. My clothes were getting a bit snug, so I decided to throw on my PINK hoodie with black tights and a pair of tan UGG boots.

"Mookie, hurry the fuck up! I'm ready!" I yelled.

"Bitch, watch yo' mouth in front of my baby. You wanna come over after getting dicked down for three weeks straight of nothing but make-up sex with Jermaine, and you've lost all home training. We are coming though," Mookie said, laughing.

Not long after, she met me at my car. My best friend's snapback was real. She had gone back to her size in no time. I couldn't wait to experience being a mom; Mookie and Ace were so happy together.

"Which store we are starting with?" Mookie asked as we reached the mall.

"I don't know, best. I think Forever 21 has a sale on their tights. I need to buy some more because I'm not going to be wearing maternity clothes," I said as if I were already fat.

"Girl, you aren't even that big. You are being extra as hell already," Mookie said. I laughed. She was right. I had always said if I were to ever get pregnant, I would be extra as hell. That was just me though.

"I almost forgot how big this mall was," I said, looking around in awe.

"Girl, OK. I feel like I haven't been to the mall in forever," Mookie said, being sarcastic.

She was just there a few weeks ago with Ace, and she knew this damn mall like the back of her hand. It was nice to see a man take care of her this time instead of her taking care of them. Entering the double doors that led to Forever 21, I went to look at the tights, while Mookie went to the heels as usual. My best friend was a heel fanatic, and that was practically all she wore. Like now, for instance, she had on a pair of wedge heels.

"P, what do you think about these shoes!" Mookie asked, screaming from across the store.

"They a'ight!" I screamed back.

I saw Mookie look to the right of her, but I just figured she was staring at another pair of shoes.

"Bitch, what you are looking at?" Mookie asked with Maliyah on her hip.

This was not what we had come here for. Mookie was a hot head and was always ready to fight anybody who looked at her funny.

"Mookie, what..." I stopped when I looked to see who was causing problems, and it was Myasia, Jermaine's slow ass ex.

"This bitch staring at me like she gay or something. I know you like what you see," Mookie spat.

"Girl, bye. Don't nobody want yo' crazy ass. I'm not even gay. Oh, wow, look who came to save a hoe," Myasia said, looking at me.

"Bitch, shut up before I drag yo' ass like I did the last time I saw you," I said, stepping closer to Myasia.

"You might not wanna do that, baby momma. You ain't the only one who might be pregnant by Jermaine," Myasia said, rolling her eyes.

"What the fuck did you just say?" I asked.

Myasia jumped back. "Bitch, you heard me," Myasia said, turning to walk away.

Mookie pulled me back when she saw me about to punch the bitch in the back of her head. "Don't even waste your time," Mookie said.

That was weird as hell. How did she know I was pregnant by Jermaine, and what did she mean by she might be pregnant by Jermaine too? I was so upset, and I hoped Jermaine wasn't telling this bitch shit behind my back.

JERMAINE

Riding through the hood, I called a meeting at my trap house on 10th Street. I wanted to let them know that I was going to step away from the game for a little bit until my baby got here, and I would need Taedoe to take on more responsibility, but I was sure he wouldn't mind. That little nigga looked up to me, and he was one of the first little niggas I had recruited under me. I trusted him. Hell, he was doing well now, and that was why I wanted him to step in.

I decided to leave my phone in the car while I was in the trap.

"Wassup, everyone?" I said to the niggas standing around me.

"Wassup, my nigga?" everyone said in accordance.

"I just called y'all here today to let y'all know I'll be stepping down for a little bit. I have a baby on the way, and my girl don't want me out here like that, so I gotta respect that," I said.

Everyone understood that this was something I needed to do. Taedoe had no problem taking over, and I instructed him that if anything went left and he felt like he couldn't handle it, he should call me, and he agreed.

Ace thought it was a bad idea to step down because I didn't even know if Porsha's baby was mine or not, and he had a point, but I didn't feel like thinking about all that extra shit. I was just ready to get home to my girl.

When I got back to my truck, I saw I had fifteen missed calls and ten text messages from Myasia and Porsha.

What the fuck was Myasia calling me for? I had told this bitch to stop hitting me up. I still had love for her but not like I had for Porsha. That was my baby, my wife, and I was even thinking about making it official with her, but after looking at her messages, I didn't think that was an option anymore.

Bm: Why the fuck you going around telling our business to your raggedy ass ex?

Bm: Then the bitch gon' tell me she might be pregnant.

Bm: ANSWER YO' DAMN PHONE, NIGGA!

Reading Porsha's text messages, I felt anger fill my body. *What the fuck? Where did she see this duck at?* As soon as I felt like we were getting back on track, this bitch Myasia was starting shit. *Fuck.* I decided to call Myasia first because her ass would listen.

"Myasia, what the fuck, yo!" I said as soon as Myasia answered the phone.

"What, daddy?" Myasia asked as if she wasn't a tad bit upset.

"Why the fuck did you tell Porsha you might be pregnant by me? Yo' ass told me you was on birth control, and you know I ain't even fucking with you like that!" I screamed into the phone, frustrated.

"Baby, I just told her what she needed to know. I was on birth control, so I didn't lie to you. I just forgot to take my pill," Myasia said.

"Stop. Myasia. Stop calling me your baby. How you forget to take your pill, bruh?" I asked.

"How you forget to pull out, knowing you might have another baby on the way?" Myasia asked sarcastically.

"Man, shut the fuck up. You a liar. I knew I shouldn't have believed yo' hoe ass, man," I said.

"Damn, Jermaine, for real? That hurt. Deep. I was there for you when that bitch was out and laid up with another nigga. Think about that shit before you call me out my name and deny what we had," Myasia said, hanging up.

Deep down, I regretted how I had said it. Myasia was my first, but she wasn't my first love. I should've told her when we put everything on the table. I just couldn't watch her cry. I knew when a nigga fucked up, it hurt the most. I couldn't believe this bitch, man. She was really trying to trap me. I didn't even know how to explain this to P. I wasn't trying to hurt Myasia, but this bitch had some shit up her sleeve, and I wasn't fucking with it. I'd known her since middle school, so I knew she had some bullshit up her sleeve. I just hoped I hadn't really gotten her pregnant. This could be the end of P and me if I had.

I called my brother, Ace, because he was the only person who could give me advice right now. Waiting for him to answer, I hoped Mookie hadn't spoken to him first, or that would really make me hot. Everybody knew Mookie couldn't hold water.

"Hey, bro. I fucked up bad," I told Ace.

"I know, my nigga. I told you not to step out of the game. Porsha needs to prove herself to you too. I love her like a sister, but she out here fucking," Ace said.

"No, Ace, it ain't even about that, It's about Myasia, man. I nutted in her. Remember I told you that? And she saw P and Mookie at the mall and told them she might be pregnant too," I said.

"Wait, what? Nigga, why the fuck didn't you tell Porsha from the jump? What the fuck was you on?" Ace asked, shocked as hell.

"Yeah, man, I fucked up. I should've told her. It looked even worse with Myasia telling her. I'm putting too much on Porsha, and she's pregnant. What should I do?" I said.

"Tell Myasia you are taking her to get a plan B, and tell Porsha what really happened," Ace said.

Plan B had never crossed my mind, especially considering we had sex more than two weeks ago. So, I knew for a fact a Plan B wasn't going to do me any justice. I wanted a baby, and what if the one

Porsha was having wasn't mine? But then again, I didn't even want a baby with Myasia. I couldn't be obligated to her delusional ass for the rest of my life.

"A'ight, bro, I'ma take care of that. Thanks for being here, my nigga," I said.

"Yeah, no problem, bro. Keep your dick in your pants for the time being," Ace said, laughing.

We both ended the call. He was right. I needed to stop fucking and get shit under control. This was what happened when you thought with your other head. I'd make it right with my baby though. I had no choice.

Porsha

I couldn't believe Jermaine hadn't returned any of my calls. He was really out here in the streets and talking about what we had going on behind closed doors. I felt so disrespected. I didn't even want to shop anymore. This nigga and his bird brain bitch had just made me look stupid once again.

"Mookie, I'm ready to go," I said, damn near about to cry.

"Girl, I know damn well you ain't 'bout to cry over this lame ass shit," Mookie said.

"No, man," I said, fighting back the tears. I really didn't want her to see me crying.

"Good, because this ain't on you, regardless of the situation. Momma always said two wrongs don't make a right, so Jermaine shouldn't be out here fucking, let alone nutting in bitches," Mookie said.

"You right, Mookie. I'm just hurt. Now he not even calling me back. I'm ready to speak to his ass. Let's go!" I said. Mookie didn't disagree. She knew I wasn't in the best position to be in this mall like this, especially after the scene that had just been caused, and everyone was now staring at us.

"What the fuck y'all looking at!" Mookie screamed, causing everyone to go back to their business. That was why I loved Mookie; she was always there when I needed her to be.

I should have known something was wrong because Jermaine was too nice this morning like he was trying to make up for something. Now it all made sense, but I wanted to get to the bottom of it once and for all. *If* we were going to be together, then he would have to cut all this lying shit out because this was too much. There was no way I should be stressing like this.

"Mookie, I don't even want to be here when Jermaine arrives," I said, pulling into our driveway.

"P, you can't run from every situation. You at least need to give him the opportunity to explain," Mookie said.

"No, I don't owe that nigga shit. I gave him a chance to air all his dirty ass laundry, and he decided to keep that a secret, so he gotta give some type of fuck about the bitch," I said.

We had just made things right a few hours ago. That dusty ass bitch had the audacity to come at me like that, which meant Jermaine had let her get comfortable, so I blamed him. He never knew when to quit. All I asked was that he be faithful, and he couldn't even do that. I knew what I had done hadn't made the situation any better, but

"P, you did some hoe shit too though," Mookie said.

"And, bitch, I ain't no liar either. I keep my shit all the way hot. I don't even want to be here when this nigga gets here for real. I'm done with him," I spat as I walked out the door.

When I got to the motel, I felt a sense of happiness, walking into the freshly cleaned room. I lay on the bed, and my mind immediately went into overdrive. Jermaine really had some nerve after all that "I love you" bullshit this morning. I knew I shouldn't have fallen for his ass in the first place. He wasn't for me. Hood was, and I just needed to face the facts.

I was so angry, so I picked up my phone and dialed his number, and when he answered, I was thrilled.

"Hey, baby, wassup?" Hood answered.

"Hi, Hood. What are you doing? Are you dressed?" I asked.

"Nothing. I was just waiting for you to call, and no, I'm not, but I can be. What about you?" Hood asked.

"Nothing. Just chilling in my motel room. You wanna come over?" I asked.

"I sure do. Not tryna sound thirsty or nothing," Hood said, and we both laughed.

"I'll text you my room number," I said.

When Hood came over, I was so excited to be with him. He seemed like the only one in my circle who understood me. Hood was dressed in a crisp white T-shirt with a pair of cool gray Nike sweat shorts and all-white G-Fazos. He also had a thin gold chain around his neck and a matching bracelet. Damn, even when he wasn't trying to dress, he dressed well.

"Hey, baby girl. What made you call me over?" Hood asked, sitting on the bed.

"I just wanted to talk and tell you what happened today," I said.

"What happened?" Hood asked.

"Well, I'ma be real with you, Hood. This only hurt me because I was planning on getting back with Jermaine. I was at the mall with Mookie, and I see Jermaine's ex-girlfriend Myasia; mind you, me and this bitch been had it out for each other just off the strength that I was fucking with Jermaine heavy, and she felt like he left her for me. So her and my best friend get into a little staring battle, and I walk over to intervene because Mookie had her baby with her. Guess what this bitch Myasia said when she seen me," I said, now getting mad all over again.

"What did she say?" Hood asked as if he wanted me to continue.

"She fucking told me she might be pregnant by Jermaine too," I said, crying, this time not even trying to hold back my tears. I was really hurt now.

Hood could tell that shit really hurt me.

"Calm down, ma. Look. I already told you, you deserve better than that, but I can't make you change your mind," Hood said, pulling me in for a hug.

"Hood... I don't feel good," I said. I started to feel lightheaded. The room began spinning, and my knees began to feel weak. Hood immediately called 9-1-1 while trying to keep me awake. When the ambulance got there, they put me on a stretcher and took me to the hospital.

"What's going on?" I asked the paramedic.

"Ma'am, are you pregnant?" she asked.

"Uh, yeah. I just found out. Why? My baby is okay, right?" I asked.

"Ma'am, I can't say for sure, but you've lost a lot of blood. I think you may be having a miscarriage," she said.

Those words echoed through my head as if they were bouncing off the inside of a cave. *A miscarriage?* This couldn't be true.

I cried the whole way to the hospital. I needed to get in contact with Mookie or someone. I was all alone, and I needed someone here with me. Being assisted to a room, I couldn't help but cry. I was pretty sure I had makeup everywhere. Today was just a fucked-up day for me.

"What happened, Porsha? They wouldn't tell me anything, because I'm not your husband or relative," Hood stated angrily as he walked into the room. I couldn't even open my mouth to speak. It was like my throat was holding my words. I shook my head and rubbed my stomach. Hood quickly walked up next to me and grabbed me, and I cried so much, and I got snot on his shoulder.

"I'm sorry," I said, laughing and backing away.

"It's all good, ma," Hood said, damn near looking like he was about to cry. I looked up and saw Jermaine and Mookie walking into the room. Hood turned around and stood up straight. Both of them pulled their guns out and aimed them at each other.

"Nigga, what the fuck you are doing here?" Jermaine asked, slipping his finger on the trigger.

"No, nigga, what the fuck you are doing here?" Hood asked.

"Jermaine, calm down. You ain't tryna do all this right here, my nigga," Ace said.

"Nigga, you lucky we in this hospital right now. I would kill you, but that would just make me a bitch ass nigga if I killed you where they would have the opportunity to save your life. When I shoot, my nigga, I shoot to kill," Jermaine said, walking over to me.

I sat there in silence. It was just like Jermaine to come to the hospital and turn up. I didn't even know how to feel. Mookie walked over to me and gave me a hug.

"Best, you OK?" Mookie asked.

"I will be, I think. How did y'all know I was here?" I asked.

"Well, you know I'm your emergency contact, best, so when you weren't answering your phone and I got the call you were at the hospital, I told Ace, and he told Jermaine, and we all rode up here together. If I knew Hood was here, I wouldn't have told them," Mookie said sincerely.

I knew she hadn't meant to cause conflict. I should've at least called her back and let her know where I was going, but I didn't want to make things complicated, but now they were really complicated. I had Hood and Jermaine in a hospital room at a very detrimental time.

"Ms. Wallace, there are too many people in the room, and some will need to leave and wait in our waiting room. Only two at a time until you are discharged," the nurse said, walking in.

Fuck, she really had to come in here and say that shit right now?

Hood and Jermaine looked at me like their lives depended on my answer, but I just sat there as they stared at me, and Mookie spoke up.

"OK, well, let's make this easy. I'm the only one staying in here, so y'all can leave," Mookie said.

I was glad she had spoken up because I didn't want to be left to make that decision. Honestly, I didn't know who I would choose. I was so thankful for Hood being in the room with me. When they left the room as Mookie had instructed, I was happy I could talk to her alone.

"Thank you for doing that, Mookie," I said.

"Girl, you know I got you. Now, tell me what happened, best," Mookie said.

"When I left the house, I was mad as hell and wanted to get far away. When I arrived at the motel, I invited Hood over. We didn't do anything this time, I promise, but I called him and not you because I felt like he was the only one I could talk to outside of you. I was ranting to him about Jermaine's no-good ass when I started feeling light-headed. Next thing I know, I'm in the ambulance, and they said I had a miscarriage."

The word miscarriage was so delicate to me now. Before, that shit didn't mean anything to me, because I'd never experienced it, but now I was afraid of it. It hurt me so bad not to have Jermaine to go to. I wished he was there, but now, I wasn't even feeling him. I kept thinking about him sleeping with that bitch, fucking her the way he fucked me. I blamed this shit on him. He caused me to lose my baby, and I didn't think I could forever forgive him. I was going to make Jermaine pay for this bullshit.

"P, I'm sorry I wasn't there for you, man. I hate myself so much for that. I'm sorry you had to meet your baby this way. I'm just glad you're good, man. I'll be here for you the rest of the way, no matter what, because if anything would've happened to you, I would've died," Mookie cried.

I hugged her because with the move I was about to make, I needed her by my side regardless of who it affected. I was tired of letting my emotions control me. I wanted to be in charge; no more naïve, simple-minded Porsha. It was time to turn my savage up.

CHAPTER SEVENTEEN

Porsha

It felt so good being released from the hospital. I didn't even want to think about that shit anymore. Remembering Jermaine and Hood watching me walk out of the hospital alone was satisfaction. I probably should've been spending more time with my family, but at this point, fuck everyone except my best friend. It was time to focus on me.

A FEW WEEKS had gone by, and I was tired of paying for the room, but I didn't want to go back home just yet, so I was thinking of a master plan. I didn't even want a relationship anymore; I wanted to be by myself. I really wanted to go out, just not alone, but Mookie was on mommy duty. I almost felt defeated until I recalled seeing a bar downstairs in the lobby.

Earlier in the week, Mookie had brought a few outfits to my room, and her exact words were, "I figured you needed to wash your ass and change your clothes, looking like two weeks ago." I laughed at the thought. She was always making jokes.

I jumped in the shower and let the steaming hot water run down my spine as I thought about my little baby. He or she was now in heaven with Glam-ma now. Sometimes I found myself thinking about my baby so much, and I didn't even notice when the tears began to flow. I dried off and moisturized my body then slipped into my VS bra and panty set.

Looking through the clothes Mookie had brought me, I decided to put on a fitted black dress that revealed just enough cleavage. I slid on my Red Bottoms, grabbed my MK clutch, and headed down to the lobby. I felt a little overdressed for the bar, but it felt great to feel like myself again. Reaching the motel lobby, I noticed there weren't many people there, but I didn't care. Hell, at least the bartender would see me. Approaching the bar, I was ready to place my order.

"I'll have a—" I was saying but was soon interrupted by a fine ass light-skinned nigga who had to have Dominican in his bloodline. His curly hair was pulled back, and he had a fresh taper around his hairline.

"Whatever she wanna order, it's on me," he said.

"I don't need you to buy me anything," I said in a flirty but stern tone.

"Nah, you don't, ma, but I'm going to anyways," he said, licking his lips.

"Well, since you insist," I said.

Damn, he was fine as hell. He was about six four, didn't have much hair on his face besides his thick ass sideburns, his smile was to die for, and I could play in his curly hair all night long if he let me. I couldn't keep my eyes off him, and apparently, he had noticed.

"You gonna stare at me all night, or are you gonna speak?" he asked.

"Well, I guess you at least deserve that much since you did buy my drink," I said, rubbing the rim of my glass.

I hadn't had sexual intercourse in a little over a month, and I was well overdue for some new meat. His demeanor was so sexy, and he carried himself like he had money, and money was what made my world go around. He favored Hood so much it was a little scary, but maybe I was just tripping.

"Yeah, you do at least owe me some conversation, ma," he said.

"Well, let me start by asking your name. I sure wouldn't want to address you as this fine light-skinned nigga I met at the bar," I said.

We both laughed.

"My name is King, but I wouldn't mind being addressed as the fine light-skinned nigga," he said cockily.

I laughed. "Boy, bye," I said.

After my fourth shot, I was all over him, and he didn't resist. I made the first move and grabbed his upper leg, trying to feel his manhood, which wasn't hard to find. Right there at the bar, it was getting hot and heavy.

"Let's go upstairs, ma," he said.

I didn't debate his suggestion, because I wanted him now. The sexual attraction was definitely there. When we reached my room door, I couldn't help but turn around and kiss him. He kissed me back and grabbed my key from me, sliding the card in and unlocking the door. King picked me up, and I wrapped my legs around him, feeling him poking through his pants.

"Damn, girl, you sexy as hell," King moaned in my ear, turning me on even more.

"I want you to fuck me, King," I moaned as he laid me on the bed and pulled my dress over my head.

"That's exactly what I'ma do," King said, pulling my panties to the side, sucking my dripping wet clit with his full, pink lips.

"Ooohh, ohhhh, King, don't stop," I moaned.

This nigga was eating me out with his gold teeth in, and that shit drove me wild. I'd never had a nigga do that to me before. I guess Mookie was right; every nigga you fucked taught you something new.

King was fully naked, and his chest, back, and arms were

completely covered in tattoos. There was something about a man with tattoos that turned me on. King put his right hand on my left breast and began massaging it while eating my pussy at the same time.

"Oh my God, I'm about to cum, K-King," I said.

"Don't cum yet," King demanded.

Something told me to try to hold it in because he had something more in store for me. King got up and revealed his manhood, which stood at attention, ready to do its job. I wasn't going to lie; I was a little scared because he was much larger than I'd expected. I lay there with my legs wide open, ready for him, and he climbed on the bed and stuck the tip in first.

"Come on, King. Don't tease me," I moaned.

"I don't think you ready for this, baby girl," King said.

"I'm tired of the foreplay, King. Just fuck me already," I whined.

This nigga really had me begging, something I've never done before because that shit was never that deep to me before. King grabbed my hand and put it on his dick, and I followed his lead. King stroked inside me deep, hitting my G-spot, causing me to cum numerous times in one round.

"Let's trade positions," I said, climbing on top of King. I rode him from the back, allowing him to watch my ass bounce up and down on his dick.

"Oh shit, ma," King moaned.

I bounced up and down, going harder until he nutted in the magnum condom. That was the best dick I'd ever had. It was good switching places with Mookie for a little bit. All my life, I had been focusing on what other people thought about me and protecting other people's feelings, and I forgot to put myself first. I blamed myself for never really experiencing life, but I sure as hell was now. I lay there breathlessly, looking at King as he did the same.

"I hope you don't think I'm some hoe, King. Really, that's not me," I said—my favorite line when I had just done some hoe shit.

"Nah, ma, I couldn't even think that if I wanted to. The way you just put it down on me, girl, I ain't even tryna see you do that for nobody else," King said.

"As long as we on the same page. Nigga, that was the Henny. Do you think you could last that long sober?" I asked sarcastically.

"Sober me and Henny me are two different things, but the dick still the same. Ms. I'm Over the Foreplay." King laughed.

"Not my fault your dick is great," I said.

"You right, but I'm tryna give it to you and only you forever," King said.

This nigga was really pushing it. Don't get me wrong; he was fine as hell, but I wasn't trying to fall for another nigga right now, especially since I barely knew him. Was his real name even King?

KING HAD TALKED me into spending more time with him. He was wining and dining me like I'd never been before. He seemed to have way more money than Hood but about equal to Jermaine. My phone was constantly going off because Jermaine felt the need to hit me up every day as if he were going to get a response. I was tired of giving chances, and I was having a great time with King. I was surprised that Hood wasn't on my line as much as usual, but I knew Jermaine wasn't giving up. That was what happened when you realized you lost something good.

"Babe, let's go out to eat tonight," I said to King.

"Where do you wanna go, baby girl?" King said.

"IHOP?" I said almost as a question because King didn't look like the type of nigga to eat at IHOP.

"Is that your favorite restaurant or something?" King asked.

Sometimes this nigga could be so bourgeois. After staying in the room for a few nights, King took me back to the house he was staying in. His home was so nice. He had a seven-bedroom, four-and-a-half-bathroom house, and it had so much space. It felt amazing being able to walk around with no panties on every now and then. I couldn't do that at Mookie's house at all unless I was in my bedroom.

King was born and raised in California, and he had come down here to expand his drug business. He already owned a majority of the west coast, and he was here to make more money. Unlike Jermaine, King didn't need my assistance. Although I missed the game, I wanted a nigga to take care of me for a little while. King had one older brother named Marcus and a baby sister named Chaquoya. I hadn't met them yet, and I damn sure wasn't in a rush. I liked things the way they were going.

King was part of a long history line of drug dealers, and it had damn near been passed down from generation to generation. His dad was locked up, serving eighteen years in the state prison in California, and he had two more years left. King was left to take over the business, and although he was the middle child, his dad thought he was the most educated on the game.

"No, nigga, I just prefer eating cheaper than going all out. Shit, unless you want me to cook," I said.

"Cook? I didn't even know you could cook," King said.

"Duh, nigga. I done told you numerous times I'm not them little bitches you been fucking with," I said, rolling my eyes.

"Well, shit, I gotta taste for steak, baked potatoes, and broccoli and cheese," King said.

"OK, you buy it, I'll cook it," I said, confident as hell. Everyone loved my cooking, so I knew he would too.

While King went into the grocery store, I decided to call Mookie. I missed my best friend. She finally answered the phone on the third ring. "P! Oh my God, I have so much to tell you, bitch," Mookie said.

"Wassup, Mookie? I miss you, bitch," I said.

"I miss you too. We definitely need to get up whenever you decide to get out of that raggedy ass motel," Mookie said.

I hadn't talked to Mookie since she dropped my clothes off at the room a few week ago, so she didn't know I was seeing someone else. She was right though; we did need to hang out.

"Girl, we really do. I miss yo' ass. I just wanted to call and check on you and tell you that I'm seeing somebody else. I met him here at the motel," I said.

"Bitch, it's barely been a month, and you moving on already," Mookie said.

"Bitch, I don't have time to be sitting around, waiting for no dumb ass nigga. I'm happy. Tomorrow, we can go out to the club if you want. You know ladies get in free before midnight. Try to get a babysitter," I said.

"I'm just looking out for you, hoe. The roles have flipped. I'm Momma P now, and you are Mookie Nasty. But yes, I'll let Ace's momma watch Maliyah. She said she wouldn't mind if I ever needed a break," Mookie said.

"OK, best, that's cool. We can just meet at the club if you want. I know Jermaine still be hanging around yo' crib, and I don't wanna see him," I said, laughing at her comment about us switching roles.

"A'ight, best, I'll call you tomorrow when I'm on my way to drop Maliyah off," Mookie said. I hung up as King finally walked back to the car, and he was looking sexy as hell. King jumped inside his all-white Range Rover, and since his windows were darkly tinted, when he opened the car door and saw me playing with myself, he didn't know how to act.

"Damn, ma, you couldn't even wait for me?" King asked, licking his lips.

"No, daddy, I couldn't," I moaned.

This nigga really brought the freak out of me. I loved the person I was becoming. I didn't want a nigga for shit but dick, and King was doing a pretty good job of supplying that. He seemed like he wanted more from me, but I wasn't interested in all that, and he knew that.

"Let me do something for you, King," I purred.

He didn't stop me, so I got on my hands and knees in the passenger seat and stuck the tip of King's shaft into my mouth, sucking it like it was a bubblegum lollipop, and I just wanted to get to the center.

"You like that, daddy?" I asked, watching King lean his head back.

"Mmmm... don't stop, P. I'm 'bout to nut," King said.

"Don't let me stop you. You can nut in my mouth," I moaned.

While deepthroating King's dick, I felt thick slime going down my throat as I swallowed him whole. I wiped the corners of my mouth and smiled with satisfaction.

King looked at me and said, "Damn, girl, I could marry you."

"Don't say shit you don't mean," I said.

"Nah, ma, that's facts," King said.

He was beginning to throw too many hints that he wanted me to be his lady, but I wasn't ready for all that, and he'd better act like he knew that. Don't get me wrong; I really liked King. He was a hustler, and he knew how to keep shit low-key, but relationships weren't for me. Period.

Later that night, once I started cooking, I couldn't help but admire his kitchen. Everything was stainless steel. His stove was a flat-top, and his refrigerator had an ice maker. *Only white people have those,* I thought. Being in his kitchen brought up memories from my childhood. We had an old ass stove with 3D eyes, and only two of them worked. That didn't stop my momma from cooking though. She cooked her ass off, and she always made a big Sunday dinner after church. Before I went off to college, my mom still had the same appliances in her house, including the big block TV. King and I sat at the table, and I let him take a bite of his food first. I wanted to see how he liked it.

"Mmmm, damn, baby, this shit tastes so good," King said.

"I knew you would like it. Told you I'm a pro in the kitchen," I said. Soon after, we finished our food, and I was good and ready for bed.

"Baby, I'm sleepy," I told King as I watched him put the dishes in the dishwasher.

"Let's go to bed then," King said.

Following King upstairs to this room, I couldn't wait to feel his soft mattress under me. I lay on the bed, and King wrapped his arms around me. We didn't want a relationship, but we acted like it. It was good having his company. Kissing King goodnight, I drifted off to sleep.

PORSHA

I woke up to the smell of bacon coming from the kitchen. King always woke up before me so he could make me breakfast. I hadn't noticed that he was such an early bird.

Running downstairs to the kitchen, I found King was shirtless, and his eight-pack was on full display.

"Whatcha making?" I asked in a childlike voice.

"Good morning, babe. I'm making bacon, eggs, sausage, grits, and waffles," King said.

"Nigga, what you want?" I asked.

"Why I always gotta want something from you just to be doing right by you?" King asked.

"Because I'm not used to this type of shit. That's why," I said, rolling my eyes.

"Well, get used to it. What do you have planned for today, baby girl?" King asked.

"Don't tell me that, but I was planning on going to the club with Mookie," I said.

"Well, I'm going with you. You don't need to be out here by yourself," King said, sounding overprotective. It wasn't even that type of party, but I was sure Mookie wouldn't mind meeting my new boo.

"I guess it wouldn't hurt for you to come," I said to King.

"Yeah, it won't," King replied.

We sat around the house all day, and King made a couple of phone calls back home to make sure everything was still running smoothly. It was. I really hoped Mookie liked King because the last thing I needed was for her to be Team Jermaine, because I was done with that nigga. Later that night, I dressed in my new two-piece, fitted Gucci set that King had bought me. The shirt revealed my cleavage so much; I almost didn't want to wear it, but he insisted. I was definitely feeling myself with a fresh deep-wave curl installation that looked so natural. I placed my 3D mink lashes on my eyelids, and you couldn't tell me shit. As I stepped into my all-black heels, I was now fully dressed and ready for tonight's events.

I looked over at King, and he dressed in an all-white True Religion outfit. He had cocaine white pants to match his white True Religion T-shirt. His all-white ensemble complimented his skin so well, and the gold accessories—a gold chain with the word "Plug" attached and a gold bracelet—pulled the outfit together nicely.

"Damn, I could do you right here," I said to King.

"The feeling is mutual, ma, the way those pants hugging yo' ass," King said. I was flattered. King was always throwing me compliments.

We were ready to go, so I quickly shot my best friend a text once we got inside King's car. As we rode down the backroads, taking the quickest route to the club, "All Of A Sudden" by Lil Baby and Moneybagg Yo blasted from the speakers.

Me: Mookie, we're on the way to the club. King is getting a booth on the second floor.

Mookie didn't reply, and I wasn't expecting her to. She was probably adding the finishing touches to her outfit. When we arrived, King automatically went to the "cut line" and paid for both of us to get in and for the booth. I'd never been in a booth before. Well, not my own booth.

Once we reached the booth, King ordered a large bottle of Remy Martin and black Hennessy. I wasn't really a drinker, because I knew it would lead to some wild sex. Taking my second shot, I saw Mookie walk through the door, but my mood quickly changed when I saw Jermaine and Ace behind her.

What the fuck? Mookie was always doing some extra shit. King saw my mood change.

"Ma, you good?" King asked.

"Yeah, I'm fine, baby. I just saw my stupid ass ex, and I don't want any parts," I said.

"You won't have to worry about none of that," King said, flashing his gun.

"Nigga, I don't want you to kill him. How did you get that in here?" I asked King.

"Connections. Just go back to enjoying your night. I got you," King said.

To my surprise, Mookie came up to our booth alone. "Hey, best, let's turn up," Mookie said.

"OK, bitch, wait. King, this is Mookie, my best friend. Mookie, this is King," I said, introducing the two.

"Damnnnn, bitch, he is fine as hell. Up-the-fuck-grade," Mookie said, adding emphasis to the word *upgrade*. I laughed and handed her a shot, and before I knew it, we were sloppy drunk. I didn't care though, because King said he had me, and I knew he meant that.

"Baby, excuse me. I gotta pee bad. I'll be right back," I said.

"A'ight, go ahead, and take Mookie with you," King said.

Little did he know, Mookie was coming with me anyway because I needed to know why the hell she had invited Jermaine and Ace here without telling me. I had a bad feeling, but I couldn't expect much, because Mookie couldn't keep a secret to save her life, and I knew that. When I finally reached the bathroom, something told me to look toward the men's bathroom, and there stood Jermaine and Ace. I knew this day was coming, but I wanted so badly for it not to be tonight.

"What the fuck are y'all staring at?" I asked, looking in Jermaine's and Ace's direction.

"Porsha, I can't believe you think you 'bout to just cut me off and not let me explain myself about that shit with Myasia," Jermaine said.

"Jermaine, I'm really not here for all that. You shouldn't have fucked the bitch, or should I say, you shouldn't have gotten the bitch pregnant," I spat.

"P, you gotta believe me, man. It wasn't nothing like that. I love you, man," Jermaine said with sincerity in his voice.

"No you don't! Stop saying that!" I screamed.

King ran down the steps from the booth, heading in my direction. "What's wrong, baby girl? You good? These niggas bothering you?" King asked.

"No, baby, this is just my ex I was telling you about," I said. King stepped closer to Jermaine, and I felt the tension and animosity.

"My girl ain't tryna be bothered, so back the fuck up 'fore I blow yo' ass back," King said.

"Nigga, yo' girl? Who the fuck are you?" Ace asked.

"I'm her man, like the fuck I said. Anybody got a problem with that?" King asked.

Mookie and I just stood there, watching everything unfold. I wasn't King's girl, but I did want Jermaine out my face because I was so done with him. I'd done my dirt, but fuck him. He had lied to me. I pulled Mookie and King away from the heated argument before it got ugly.

"Just know if I can't have you, nobody will," Jermaine said, walking away.

What the fuck did he mean by that? That's why I didn't fuck with his ass like that, always demanding shit, thinking if he kills somebody, he'll get his way.

I tried to enjoy the rest of my night by pouring numerous shots of liquor, damn near drinking the whole bottle. Hennessy was the devil's drink, but I loved the way it made me feel. I grabbed King and kissed him passionately.

"Let's go to the bathroom and fuck," I whispered in King's ear sexily.

"Damn, girl, you just surprise me more and more every day with that freaky shit. You sure you tryna do all that?" King asked.

"Yes, daddy, I'm sure. I want you to fuck me though. You take charge," I moaned in King's ear.

Mookie stood in the booth, dancing with some nigga, so she didn't mind staying there while we went for a quickie.

"I'm having so much fun, best," Mookie said. I looked at her and smiled. My best friend hadn't been out since she had been on mommy duty. Apparently, Ace and Mookie had an open relationship; she was kissing all over a random man.

"Mookie, don't turn up too much. I'll be right back," I said. Heading to the bathroom, I could barely walk, but King was right there, holding me up.

"Excuse me, ladies. Can y'all clear the bathroom?" King asked.

Everyone did as they were told, and King locked the door so no one else could get in. King walked over to me, kissing me on the lips, and I felt myself getting wetter.

"Fuck me, King," I said, pulling his pants down.

King pulled my pants down and picked me up, and I wrapped my legs around his waist as he began to fuck me.

"You love this dick?" King asked, moaning in my ear.

"Yesss, daddy, I do," I said.

King was going hard, pounding my little kitty, and I didn't want him to stop.

"Don't cum yet. I'm not done," King said, turning me on even more.

I did as I was told. King always told me to hold my release, which ended up making me cum even more. King went down on me while I was lying across the sink. This man really brought the freak out of me. The only place I'd ever had sex with Jermaine and Hood was in their damn bedroom. Now here I was, bent over a sink, getting my shit pounded from the back in the club. King lasted a long time since he was gone off the Henny. Then he pulled out and released himself in the sink.

"Damn, bae, you don't be playing, do you? That Henny dick never disappoints." I giggled.

"Hell nah. With you, I ain't got time to play," King said.

"I'm ready to go home, King," I said.

I wanted to say goodbye to Mookie before I left. Before leaving the bathroom, I freshened up and headed back upstairs to the booth with King behind me. When I walked back up to the booth, Mookie was sitting there and taking another drink to the head.

"Best, slow down," I said.

"Bitch, I-I'm grown," Mookie said, stuttering. I could tell my best friend was too drunk, and I wasn't about to leave her like that with that random nigga.

"Come on, Mookie. Let's go," I said.

"Wait, where are Ace and Jermaineeeeeee?" Mookie asked, dragging his name out.

"Girl, I don't know, and I don't give a fuck. I'll just drop you off at home. They'll see you when you get there," I said. Mookie got up, damn near knocking everything off the tables in our booth. "Come on, girl. Let's go," I said.

Walking near the exit, I felt a funny feeling in my stomach again like something was about to happen, but I wanted to make it to the car. I would feel so much more secure if I could just make it to the car. Damn near carrying Mookie's drunk ass, I looked behind me to make sure King was still there, and he was.

As we were finding our way through the crowd, I heard someone yell, "He's got a gun!"

I looked around with fear in my eyes. I didn't see anyone, but I wasn't ready to die. I ran out of the club, dragging my friend behind me. King had his gun out, aiming it in the crowd to be sure he was the first one to shoot if need be because he didn't want Mookie, me, or himself to get hurt. Before I knew it, Ace, Jermaine, and Tadoe shot in our direction. What the fuck was he thinking? This nigga was really a fucking psycho.

Bullets were flying through the air, and everybody was screaming. I just tried my best to maneuver through the crowd. I lost Jermaine and King. Mookie damn near had a panic attack from screaming so loud. My adrenaline was pumping. If I had a gun, I swore I would have shot Jermaine, not to kill but just to scare his ass. Was this what he meant by if he couldn't have me, then nobody would? What did I get myself into? I was starting to get nervous. Where was King? I had made it all the way back to the car, and he was nowhere to be found.

"Best, where is King?" Mookie asked.

"I don't know, man. I need to go back and find him," I said.

"Well, you aren't going alone, bitch. Come on," Mookie said. Running through the crowd, I saw an all-black Tahoe swerve away from the scene. The car looked exactly like Jermaine's car, and my mind immediately went into overdrive.

Oh my gosh! Oh my gosh, I hope King is OK. Why did I get him in the middle of my shenanigans? I would feel so guilty if something happened to him even if I wasn't the one to pull the trigger.

Walking near the exit of the club where Jermaine was shooting, I couldn't believe my eyes. King was laid out with a gunshot wound to the chest.

"What the fuck! Oh my God, no! No, no, King, baby, stay with me, please," I cried out. Every fucking time something was going well for me, something always got in the way of my happiness. I took my shirt off, not giving a fuck who saw me. I wanted to save my man.

"Call 9-1-1! What are y'all standing around for!" Mookie yelled.

When the ambulance arrived, they said King had lost a lot of blood. I was so upset. I didn't want Jermaine near me. I guess he thought by doing this dumb shit, I would take him back. He'd better hope like hell King did make it. That was a nightmare.

"Best, I can't believe Jermaine and Ace. I'm so sorry for bringing them, man. I didn't know shit was going to go left like this," Mookie said.

"It's OK, best. You didn't even know King was coming. Mookie, me and this man both agreed that we didn't want a relationship, but he was protecting me like he wanted more. I was never too sure with him," I said.

"He seems like he's just your type, P. He got money, and you have someone taking care of you for once," Mookie said.

———

Hours had passed, and Mookie was spread out across the chairs with her head in my lap. I sat waiting for the doctors to come out and tell me something. I couldn't stop thinking about King. He was what I wanted, but we were both being stubborn.

"Is there family here for King?" the doctor came out and asked. I stood up, damn near knocking Mookie onto the floor.

"Yes, I'm here," I said, walking toward the doctor.

"Ma'am, who are you to the victim?" the doctor asked.

"I'm his girlfriend. I was with him tonight at the club. Please tell me he's OK," I cried.

"Ma'am, we retrieved the bullet from his chest. He's a really lucky man. It was exactly four centimeters away from his heart. He is in a coma right now, but we are expecting him to wake up within the next few weeks with the proper medication," the doctor said.

A coma? A fucking coma? Are you serious?

"Thank you so much for everything, doctor. When will I be able to see him?" I asked with a sense of relief.

"I'll take you to his room right now. We have him in a protected unit so no one can get in and harm the patient. If your friend wants to come, she can. It's only supposed to be immediate family, but you're the only ones here for him, so why not?"

Walking down the silent, cold hallway, I was so happy that King was good, and they expected him to wake up within the next few weeks. When we approached the room, King looked so different. I stood in the doorway with tears in my eyes.

"Mookie, I can't handle this," I said.

"No, bitch, yes you can. If you can't, that's what I'm here for," Mookie said, grabbing me for a hug.

I wept in my best friend's arms. I felt so useless. I had tried to leave this nigga Jermaine alone, but he just wouldn't let me be happy with someone else. Sitting there, looking at King with cords hooked up to him, I really couldn't believe I had caused all of this. When King woke up, I knew there would be war all over again because King was the type of nigga to get even, and I wasn't prepared for whatever he had in store.

"P, we gotta go home and get dressed. My baby is still at Ace's momma's house since Ace didn't go get her last night," Mookie said. She was right. We did need to leave, but I didn't want to leave King's side in case he woke up.

"Mookie, can you just take my car and go get me some clothes and bring them back here? I don't want to leave King alone," I said.

"Yeah, best, no problem. You know I got you," Mookie said, leaving me alone to sit with King.

Sitting there, watching him lay there, I grabbed his hand and said a prayer.

"God, I haven't spoken to you since my mom died, but I'm just trying to find some sort of guidance in my life. I don't understand, but I've been in a lot of situations I've never had to encounter before. I'm coming to you as humbly as I know how, asking you to take care of King. Let him wake up sooner than later from this coma and have a speedy recovery. Amen."

Looking toward the ceiling with tears in my eyes, I didn't know why, but I expected something to change that very moment, and when it didn't, I got frustrated. My momma always told me to pray to the Lord when I felt my weakest.

I'll always feel weak without you, Momma.

I felt my eyes getting heavy, so I decided to go lie on the couch they had in the room. I dozed off, but my phone going off woke me from my sleep.

What the fuck! I just closed my eyes. Damn.

To my surprise, it was Jermaine calling. I decided I would answer and tell that motherfucker what it was and what it wasn't.

"What the fuck you want?" I asked Jermaine.

"Damn, ma, don't be so harsh," Jermaine said.

"Jermaine, if you think shooting King was gonna make me wanna fuck with you again, you dumber than I thought you were," I spat.

"I just wanted to prove to you that what I say is what I mean. If I can't have you, then nobody can. Period. You really think after all these years we've been together, I'ma just let you go and be with another nigga?" Jermaine asked.

"It's not what you're going to let me do; I'ma grown ass woman. I'm happy with him. You couldn't even show me the attention and time I needed. Go be with Myasia," I said with anger and hurt in my voice.

I really didn't want that, because I knew what Jermaine was capable of, but that was how things had to be.

"I don't want that bitch. What don't you understand? Before yo' man came up last night, acting all hard and shit, I was just gon' tell you how fucked up you were. You left me as soon as you heard I fucked Myasia, but you expect me to be all good with you and Hood. And shit, now you and King. That's not how that shit works. I know you still love me; you don't even have to say it. You just fucking with that nigga to fill that void," Jermaine said. He was right. I still loved him, but I couldn't be with him.

"Jermaine, I'm done with you, and this is my last time answering your calls too," I said.

"That's cool, but this won't be the last time you see me, Porsha," Jermaine said.

I hung up. I was so over him, and the shit he had done last night was unbelievable. I needed him to let shit go. I lay back down on the couch and drifted off to sleep.

CHAPTER EIGHTEEN

Porsha

The night King was shot gave me nightmares. I was accustomed to the game, but I hadn't quite adjusted to seeing someone being shot in front of me, especially someone I really cared about. It had been three weeks now, and King hadn't woken up yet. I was beginning to get worried.

I FOUND myself sitting by King's bedside day in and day out. I really cared for him, and this accident only made me care about him more.

"Mmmmm." King made a noise, clearing his throat.

"Oh my God, baby, you're up," I said. "Somebody get a nurse or a doctor! He's up!" I screamed.

"Baby, calm down," King said, but I couldn't. It had been three long weeks, and I hadn't heard his voice or anything. I couldn't control myself.

"Hello, King. How are you feeling?" the doctor asked.

"Hi, Doc. I feel like shit actually," King said.

"Well, that's normal. I'm just going to check your lungs and breathing to make sure everything is all good," the doctor said. The doctor began checking King's respirations and blood pressure just to assure everything was normal.

"Everything sounds fine. Honestly, you're one of our patients we consider a miracle. You should be out of here in no time," the doctor said.

"Good, because I have some stuff to handle," King said jokingly but serious.

I knew he was talking about Jermaine and his boys.

Those words the doctor just said were like music to my ears. King was really strong. I didn't think I could take a bullet and survive. The doctor left the room, and I felt a sense of relief because I wanted to talk to King about what had happened the night at the club.

"Baby, I thought you were right behind me," I said.

"I was, bae, but when I saw that bitch ass nigga aiming his gun in yo' direction, I immediately went into defense mode. I'm just glad it was me and not you, baby girl," King said, gesturing for me to come sit on the bed next to him.

"I know. That nigga is a psychopath. I didn't have anything on me to protect myself, so when I ran back to the car with Mookie, I didn't see you behind me. I ran back, and there you were, laying on the ground, helpless and bleeding out. There was nothing I could do," I cried.

"Babe, don't feel like it was all you, because it wasn't. I'm going to do everything in my power to protect you. I love you, Porsha, and I'm tired of hiding it. I'm not expecting you to say it back right now, because I already know you feel for me. I mean, you did stay up here the whole time," King said.

I sat there in silence. King was right. I did feel for him, and my feelings were growing for him, but I had love for Jermaine, and I didn't want either of them beefing. But that was where I drew the line with them. They could handle it how they wanted to. I was leaving it in the streets.

KING

This nigga Jermaine didn't even know what type of nigga I was. He was shooting at the wrong motherfucker, but the night he shot at me, he ended his own life. Porsha was really a good girl, and I wasn't going to lose her to some nigga who didn't deserve her. Making a phone call to my brothers and cousins in California, I would have them here in no time. I was done wasting time; I needed to get to business. It was time to put a couple of niggas to rest.

Waiting for my big brother, Marcus, to answer the phone, I was more than ready to set something up. This time though, I would keep my hands out of the pot. That was what I had niggas under me for—to handle my lightweight.

"Wassup, bro? How you are living, my nigga?" Marcus asked.

"Nigga, we got some shit to handle. Let's cut the chit-chat," I said.

"Word? What happened down there? I told you Atlanta was crazy as hell when you first mentioned bringing business down there. How you handling shit with that nigga Jermaine and his bitch? I told you Hood wasn't solid enough to take on all that pressure," Marcus said.

"Yeah, yeah, yeah, bro, I was just trying to give that nigga a chance to make it make sense. I was mad as hell when he called me and told me he might've got her ass pregnant. I knew it was time for me to step in 'cause I'ma handle shit. I was shot a few weeks ago though, so that's why I hadn't called back. This nigga was shooting to kill because the doctor said he shot me in my chest, and the bullet was exactly four centimeters away from my heart, bro," I said.

"What the fuck! Are you serious? Why the fuck didn't you call us soon as you noticed that nigga had beef with you? I hope it wasn't behind that bitch," Marcus said.

"Nigga, I didn't even know the nigga was strapped until I walked out the damn club, and don't disrespect her like that. Can you grab everyone up and y'all niggas come down here? We got shit to handle," I said.

"Don't tell me you falling for her too. She must got some good ass pussy. But hell yeah, bro, you know you ain't said shit but a word. We on the next thing smokin', my nigga," Marcus said.

"Good to hear, bro. Once everything is in order with this nigga Jermaine, I'll send y'all back to Cali unless y'all wanna stay here with me," I said.

"We'll talk about that when I touch down, bro. I can't have you out of my sight. You way down there, and I'm way over here in Cali," Marcus said.

Even though my brother, Marcus, had some shit with him, every time I needed him, he was ready to ride. He swore every time I got into some shit with another nigga, it was behind a bitch because I was always taking nigga's bitches. I lay in my bed and watched Porsha as she slept. I was surprised she didn't hear me on the phone, but she was a hard sleeper. I hadn't been fucking with her long, but this girl had my mind gone. I saw why my cousin was down here falling off his mojo. The last bitch I fucked with was a dub, and she was fucking every nigga in Cali. Porsha had that good ass pussy that made me want to take her out the hood, somewhere on the outskirts of Atlanta where we could run this game together. If she thought she'd seen money when fucking with Jermaine, she was in for a surprise, especially once I took over his clientele.

If I didn't know anything else, I knew I was going to have this nigga Jermaine killed for trying me like a bitch ass nigga.

TO BE CONTINUED...

AFTERWORD

First and foremost I want to thank each and everyone of you for reading this book. If you're interested in my work like/follow these following pages. I really appreciate you guys thanks again!

Facebook: Precious The Authoress
Readers group: Reading with Precious T.

COMING NEXT!